BRAVE
NEW
GIRL

This book is for Sophie Outram who remade
classic films on Super 8 when she was 13.
Also thanks to Gonçagul of Mossbourne Academy,
and finally The Arts Council England.

JANETTA OTTER-BARRY BOOKS

Brave New Girl copyright © Frances Lincoln Limited 2011
Text copyright © Catherine Johnson 2011

First published in Great Britain in 2011 and in the USA in 2012 by
Frances Lincoln Children's Books, 4 Torriano Mews,
Torriano Avenue, London NW5 2RZ

www.franceslincoln.com

A catalogue record for this book is available from the British Library

ISBN 978-1-84780-254-5

Set in Palatino

Printed and bound by CPI Group (UK) Ltd, Croydon, CR0 4YY in September 2011

1 3 5 7 9 8 6 4 2

like that, up on the big screen, in a proper cinema, there is nothing like it!"

"I couldn't make film club cos I had to go and pick up Denny. His school choir was having some major rehearsals. Anyway, that Flying Thingies, wasn't it one of those fighting films?" I did my best *ninja* slice with sound effect and almost hit Miss Tunks, the drama teacher, as she passed with her tray.

"Seren Campbell Ali!" she said loudly, and half the dining room turned to look.

I felt my face going hot and pink. "I'm sorry, Miss, I never meant…" I stood up to try and help, and tripped over the table leg and nearly fell over her.

People laughed. I went redder.

Miss Tunks was angrier now. "You are so… so gauche! Keith, can you not keep an eye on your friend, please, before she does some serious damage?"

"Sorry, Miss," I mumbled. I swear that woman gave me the evil eye as she passed.

"She hates me," I said when Miss Tunks had gone. "I know she does, after last year's play and then the Christmas show! I thought Drama was supposed to be fun, now it's just torture! And what the hell does gauche mean?"

Keith shrugged. "Dunno. Maybe clumsy or

something. And you have got to admit it, you do trip over stuff. Sometimes."

"Keith! Do not remind me!" I said. I didn't want to think about last year. "I'm a different person now, OK? Completely." I took a deep breath. "I am *so* not that girl!" I shivered, remembering.

Keith shook his head. "Miss Tunks *so* doesn't hate you."

"She so does! She always puts me with Sanjay and he's rubbish. Anyway, can we forget that just happened?"

"Suits me." Keith shrugged. He took a spring roll out of his lunchbox. "I was talking about those films, yeah? Well…" He coughed. "I was thinking, you know, I might want to make films like that."

"What, *Crouching Keith, Hidden Teacher*?"

"No. Not exactly," Keith said flatly.

"Well, I wouldn't like to be there when you tell your mum you won't be East London's top accountant because you're off to Hollywood."

"I'd get my Uncle Ed to talk her round. And she'll soon change her mind when I'm walking down some red carpet or winning an Oscar."

"I don't know. Your mum has wanted you to be an accountant forever."

Keith took a piece of paper from his back pocket. "I was thinking, Seren. Miss Tunks gave me this." He laid the paper out on the table. It said: *East End Film Festival. Young Eye Film Competition.* "If you win you get shown on the big screens at the Olympic stadiums, while people are sitting down or something."

"Miss Tunks said you should enter? She must like you."

"She's all right, really. I thought I could make a film for this competition, and *you*," he pointed his spring roll at me, "could give me a hand. You in, Seren? It could be a laugh. And even if I get on the shortlist, which, OK, is a long shot, they show the films at your local cinema. My film, up on the big screen at the Rio!"

"With your name on and everything?" I said.

"With *our* names on it. It's not just my film."

I must admit I liked the idea of that. "But haven't you got to win first?" I said.

"Yeah, I know that..." Keith was off talking about lighting and angles. I started watching Sasha again, but Keith nudged me back to attention. "This Saturday, we could do some recces, talk about stuff."

"*Recces*?" I made a face.

"Recces. It means looking around. It's what film

people say. It means checking out locations."

I sighed. "I suppose I won't have anything else to do."

"It'll be a laugh. And you could look at the script. Once I've written it, that is. I mean, it doesn't need a whole long script, it's only five minutes long."

"So you don't want me to write it for you?"

"No, but I'd like your help. It's only short. But, yeah, you're great with ideas – you know you are."

I was blushing now.

"So. I'll come over to yours," said Keith firmly. "I'll tell Mum I'm at Youth Orchestra."

"Oh yeah? You'll miss Youth Orchestra? I bet you chicken out."

Keith had Chinese Saturday School in the morning followed by Youth Orchestra all afternoon. Keith's mum was always telling Keith, and anyone else who'd listen, that he was going to Business School.

"She won't be happy," I said. "And your mum…" I'd seen Keith's mum furious. She was a tiny woman who looked sweet and cuddly, but when she was angry….

"What she doesn't know won't hurt her, so this is on the down-low, OK? Whatever you do, don't mention it to your mum either. I know they talk."

I thought that since my mum was halfway through the new Jenny Darling romance, there wasn't a chance that she'd notice much of anything.

On the other side of the hall, Luke Beckford smiled and tossed his long fringe out of his light-brown eyes. Actually, that was exactly the way Jenny Darling would have written it and there, in front of me, it was happening for real. From the look on her face I reckoned Sasha's heart had triple-selkoed (I had been watching that *Celebrities on Ice* thing) into her throat, and I knew I would have to do something.

"Were you listening, Seren?" Keith said, elbowing me. "About the film and that? Seren?"

"'Course." I smiled even though I could see that Luke Beckford was leaving the dinner hall with Keely Marchant, and Sasha looked as if she'd just discovered she had FAIL stamped across her forehead in foot-high letters.

"'Course I'll help, Keith," I said. "And you can do something for me...."

★★★

I worked out the plan in the last lesson, which was IT. I also looked up the word 'gauche', which meant socially awkward and not clumsy. Miss Tunks got it *so* wrong.

Our IT teacher, Mr Choudry, always got caught up with Sanjay and Ed, who never did any work, so I could have a good think about how to get Luke and Sasha together. I explained the plan twice to Keith.

He wasn't convinced. "It's rubbish, Seren, no way is it ever going to work," he hissed at me. "What are you going to do? Apart from blackmailing Luke Beckford into asking Sasha out, I don't see how you can *make* something like that happen. It's not like you can force someone to fancy someone else, is it?"

"Not blackmail, Keith! And not forcing! It is possible. My mum reads about it all the time in her books. You just have to get the boy to see exactly what he's missing. Luke's problem is he only sees Sash in school. If he knew her better…."

"I thought you said she has loads of irritating habits, like doing those really smelly burps when she's eaten cheese-and-onion crisps, and farting in bed?"

"If I'd wanted negative I would have asked Christina!"

"And she would never have answered, even if you gave her cash."

I flicked a look over at where Christina was sitting with Ruby and Shazna. Where we used to sit before

Christmas. Before the show. I felt my skin prickling, and had to take a deep breath. There was no question – I *was* socially awkward. Miss Tunks was right.

Keith made a face. "Seren, I'm sorry, OK? I shouldn't have said that. You know me, foot in mouth."

"No, you shouldn't have."

"Go on, Seren, I'm listening. So, your sister, Sasha, and Luke Beckford…" I could see he was trying to sound more interested.

I looked at him. It was better having one true friend, I thought, than three crap ones. Keith might be a boy, but he was nothing like Ed, who had the start of a beard already, or Sanjay, who towered over all the teachers. Keith was stick thin, shorter than most of the Year Sevens and knew more about films than anyone.

"Seren?"

I'd known him since I was six, when I met him swinging his legs against the counter in the *Paradise International Food and Wine Supermarket* on our estate. Our mums got chatting and then we got chatting.

"I'm sorry." Keith drew a little smiley on the corner of my IT notebook. "It'll work," he said. "We'll make it work, OK?"

Me and Keith walked home by the canal. My little brothers, Denny and Arthur, were at after-school club and Mum had texted to say she'd pick them up after her shift driving the bus, cos Denny had some good news. I thought it must be very good news to have tempted her away from Jenny Darling's latest bestseller.

It was the second really sunny day this year and the blossom was out, and there was a family of fluffy ducklings swimming over the water towards the Olympic Park. Me and Keith watched as the mummy duck led her babies under the chain-link fence, and across the brand-new grass towards the huge, dazzling stadium that looked so new and shiny it could've landed from outer space.

"It looks unreal," I said.

"I can't imagine all the people," Keith said, staring. "My mum says we're going to clear out the spare room and rent it for a packet. It's going to be amazing, don't you think? All those people, from all over the world!"

"Never mind the Olympics! It's Luke Beckford we've got to sort out. He's got to understand that Sasha is the one for him. He goes to your shop, doesn't he?"

"Yeah, sometimes. Sundays after football on the Astroturf. He buys those energy drinks."

"Well then – we get them both in at the same time. I'll make sure Sasha's wearing something nice – not too much lip gloss – and she'll talk to him and he'll realise how pretty and everything she is...." I shut my eyes and imagined the scene. It would be like the back cover of one of Mum's romances.

It would be the first time Luke would see Sasha, like, really see her. I'd be talking to her over in the cereal aisle, and she would be cool and funny like she could be when she wasn't tongue-tied under the weight of her crush, or when her so-called best mate wasn't giggling for England. Luke would hear her from over by the big chiller and come round the corner, and time would sort of slow down.

I opened my eyes. "It's possible. I mean, if they can build all this from nothing, then getting Sasha and Luke together has got to be a breeze."

"Seren, your sister..."

"Yes? What are you saying, Keith? Are you saying she's not good enough for Luke Beckford or something?"

"No, Seren, of course I'm not. It's just, well... getting people hooked up like that, it doesn't work in real life, does it? " He looked at me seriously. "I mean, it's just a meeting in a supermarket, it's not a date, not like going to the cinema or out for a meal. I just think you shouldn't get your hopes up."

"I'll make it work. Didn't I fix it last term when my little brothers wanted to go Trick and Treating and needed outfits?"

"Yeah, but people's feelings are a load more complicated than black bin-liners…"

"I know that! Well then, didn't I sort it out when you thought you wanted to go to Summer Uni and do Media last year, and your mum wanted you to do extra Maths?"

"I know! But that's different too! Seren, you never listen."

"But Keith, I can do this too, I can make things happen, good things! I know it!"

2
GOOD NEWS

"Denny's choir's been picked for the Opening Ceremony!" Arthur, my youngest brother, ran out of the house and into my arms. He was squealing high and loud, and his five-year-old face was pink with excitement.

"Have you been at the Cherry Coke again, Arthur?" I said. I hoped not. If he had he'd be up all night bouncing off the walls and no amount of *Frog and Toad at Home* would get him off to sleep.

I had hardly walked through the door when Mum hugged me so hard I thought I was going to faint. "He's right, Seren! Our Den! Singing at the Olympics, with all the world watching!"

Denny was cramming his mouth with Iceland sausage-rolls – his favourite.

"Denny'll be famous!" Arthur said, and grinned at me.

"Isn't it fantastic?" Mum said again. She swooped on Denny and kissed the top of his head. Denny pulled away. "You're a star, Den!"

"It's not just me, Mum, it's the Year Six choir. Miss Khan said we were wonderful, and that man off the telly who did the auditions said we was wonderful too."

"So no one noticed you singing flat, then?" I said, helping myself to a sausage roll before they all disappeared into the black hole that is my biggest little brother's mouth.

"Mum!" Denny said, his voice gone from proud to whiny in seconds.

"Will you stop teasing him, Seren?"

"Oh, Den, you know I'm pleased really," I said, and he smiled again.

"All the Olympic boroughs could put forward one primary and one secondary school choir," Denny said, spraying sausage roll as he spoke.

"And it's Denny Denny Denny from Gains–borough!" Arthur was jumping up and down, Mum joined in and then we were all dancing round the kitchen, holding hands, while Denny sang his tune at top volume – *London World in One City*. We were still at it when Sasha and her mate Fay came in.

"Oh My God!" Sasha said. Fay had her hand in front of her mouth, but you could see she was practically choking, trying not to laugh. Fay was sort of all right, but it didn't help that Christina was her younger sister. I imagined she'd be double-quick to tell her all about how nuts that Seren was as soon as she got home.

Arthur ran towards her, his hands sticky with sausage roll, and she only just managed to swerve to avoid a pink'n'yellow, flaky-pastry cuddle. "Fay-ee!" he squeaked.

But they'd both gone upstairs in seconds. Mum shouted up about Denny, and Sasha shouted something back that sounded like 'great', then slammed the bedroom door.

I started clearing away the sausage-roll mess. "She should be down here," I said. "With us."

Mum turned the tap on for the washing-up. "Oh, leave her, Seren. Her and Fay have got grown-up stuff to deal with. You could always call Christina. She hasn't been round for a bit, has she?"

I changed the subject quickly. "Mum! I am grown-up too!" I said, putting a plate in the sink. "I'm 13. I read to Arthur, I do the dinner some days when you're working late. I do the laundry too! Sasha's supposed to do the ironing but she never does, she's rubbish!"

"I didn't mean that, love," Mum said. "'Course I didn't. In a lot of ways you're about five years older than Sasha. You're ten times better with the little ones, and you're great at school."

I cringed, thinking about Miss Tunks.

Mum squirted some washing-up liquid into the bowl and looked out into the back yard. "You've always been so helpful, love."

From upstairs there was the sudden blast of the RnB number one, so loud the window almost rattled in the frame.

"Oh, go and tell them to turn it down, Seren," Mum said. "How am I ever going to be able to read with that row going on?"

Upstairs, in our bedroom, Fay and Sasha were trying on false eyelashes.

"Mum says to turn it down," I said, shouting over the music and sitting down on my bed.

"What d'you reckon, Seren?" Sasha turned towards me and batted her new, improved ultra lashes.

"I think she looks gorgeous!" Fay said, batting hers back. "No surprise Luke wanted your picture!"

Sasha flushed pink.

"Did he?" I said. "Luke Beckford?" I couldn't help feeling excited for her.

"No, Luke Backwards, who d'you think?" Sasha snapped. The look she gave me could have broken mirrors.

I kept my mouth shut. I would have liked to ask Fay how Christina was doing, if she ever said anything about me. But I didn't. In the old days Fay would have been here with Christina and it would have been all of us together having a laugh. They'd do my make-up and let me join in. Now Fay and Sasha talked to each other close and low so I couldn't hear.

I had promised myself, after what happened with Christina, that everything would change. That I wouldn't let it get to me. That I'd come back to school for the spring term completely different: sorted, mature. If she didn't want to be mates any more it would be her loss, not mine. Things were different all right, but I didn't feel any more grown-up. I felt as if I was on the edge of everything, that I didn't belong anywhere. Even in my own room.

Maybe Mum was right, maybe it was just that they were older now, Sash and Fay. And it wasn't the fake eyelashes, which I had to say didn't look too mad once they'd got them on right. They'd be leaving school for good in a few months and it was a bit like they'd outgrown everything: school, me, and our tiny bedroom.

I wanted to tell both of them about what I was planning, about how Sasha would get to go to the Prom with Luke if I had anything to do with it.

I picked up a magazine, but there was nothing in it, and before I got to the worst-dressed pages Sasha said, "Seren?"

"Mmm?" I kept looking at the magazine. I didn't want to seem too desperate.

"Me and Fay were wondering if you'd do us a favour?"

I folded the magazine shut. I would have done anything.

"Would you run over to your little mate's shop and get us a Freddo each – you can get one yourself, but don't tell the boys cos they'll only want something too."

I felt my heart sink. Really sink, like the lift going all the way to the bottom level of the underground car park in Canary Wharf. This was not supposed to happen.

It used to be *us* getting rid of the boys with promises of biscuits or something on the telly. Now they were gett[...] of me. I smiled, even though I felt like I'd been hit by a netball right under the ribs. All the breath knocked out of me.

They had the laptop open and were scrolling through some clothes website online. As far as they were concerned I had practically vanished. I didn't count at all. They didn't want chocolate, they just didn't want me around.

"Don't call Keith my 'little' mate!"

For a second Sasha looked really worried. "Oh, no! You haven't fallen out with him too?"

I rolled my eyes. "No."

"Tell you what, Ser, we'll do your eyes when you come back, how about that, yeah?"

Somehow that sounded worse. It was like she was only doing it to make me feel better, cos she felt bad. I went downstairs and slammed the front door. It was still warm and little kids were running around in the car park. There was a drink can in the gutter and I kicked it hard.

One of the kids yelled at me. "Is Denny coming out?"

"I don't know!" I snapped, and he ran away as if I'd hit him.

I took a deep breath. It was no use being angry, I

knew that just made everything turn out even worse. I didn't do that sort of thing any more.

I just had to make it work with Luke and Sasha. Then maybe she'd think twice about ignoring me.

***

It rained all day Saturday. Keith texted me in the morning to say it was too wet to go and look at locations so he'd be going to Youth Orchestra after all. I texted back 'CHICKEN'.

By the time Keith did come round, it was after tea and the boys were sitting in front of the telly, watching giant dinosaurs chasing people through time.

Keith looked at me shiftily. "Can we talk?" It wasn't like him at all.

"Are you all right?" I said.

"Keeeith!" Arthur said, and threw a cushion at him.

"I'm singing in the Olympics, at the Opening Ceremony!" Denny said. The boys loved Keith. He was like an unofficial big brother.

"Fantastic!" Keith said, throwing the cushion back, gently, at Arthur. "That is great, Den, but I need to talk to Seren. Upstairs."

"Ooo-oooh!" said Denny, and Arthur sang, "Keith's your boyfriend!" over and over.

"That is so lame, boys. If you want to wind me up you'll have to try a lot harder," I said, because it was so blatantly not true. And, may I add, it never has been and what's more, the boys knew it too.

"What is it?" I said, on the way up. "Has something happened?"

"Is Sasha in?" He looked round the bedroom.

"She's not in the cupboard, Keith, honest," I said. He was looking around, nervous. "She doesn't finish work until seven." Sasha did a Saturday job, waitressing in my dad's restaurant in the afternoons.

"Good." Keith shut the door behind us. "I was at Youth Orchestra."

"I know," I said. "I didn't think you'd get out of it. You always say you'll bunk off, but your problem is you're just too good."

Keith pushed his glasses back up his nose. "I told you, it was the weather!"

I smiled. "So, am I looking at your wonder script or not?"

"It's not a script exactly – not yet. Anyway, something came up. I heard them talking at Youth Orchestra."

"Them?" I made a face. "Go on."

"There were some girls from school, from Year

Eleven, Danielle something and her mate with the short hair."

"Amy, isn't it?"

"Yeah, Amy." He nodded.

"Well?"

"I was just packing up, and I heard these girls talking... I don't always hang around girls talking, that's not my style at all."

I rolled my eyes. "Well, you're not jamming with the boys going over the football scores."

"I do. Sometimes!" Keith sounded hurt. "I only listened because they were talking about your precious Luke!"

"He's not *my* Luke!" I was practically jumping up and down. "Spit it out, Keith!"

"They said he was going out with Keisha Coates."

I let out a long breath and flopped back on the bed. I wanted to laugh, I was so relieved. "Oh my days! That news is so old it's probably carved in stone! Carved in stone on the side of a pyramid or something. Everyone knows they split up weeks ago! You had me worried there for a second, you really did."

"Are you sure?"

"I am sure. I'm surer than sure," I said. I looked at

22

him. He seemed nervous. "What is it you're worried about? Is it tomorrow? You don't want us to even try, do you?"

"No, it's just…" He sighed. "Well, yes, all right, I am worried." He took a deep breath. "I know you, Seren. It could all backfire. I'm worried you'll be disappointed."

"So? I'll be disappointed! At least I'll have tried. At least, maybe, Sasha will see I'm not entirely useless. I mean, Keith, what's the worst that can happen?"

Keith said nothing. He opened his mouth and shut it again, more than once. I knew there was a chance things might not work out – Luke might be ill with some new kind of flu, Sasha might do one of her earth-shattering burps, thinking the shop was empty – but we had to try.

"And if Luke Beckford did have a new girlfriend, I would be the second to know – maybe third, after Sasha and Fay. Believe! It's all still on for tomorrow," I said, trying to sound determined and in control. "So, now that's settled, why don't you tell me about your film?"

Keith made a face that said 'I'm still not convinced'. I made one back that said 'that's that', and he fished about in his bag and brought out a notebook.

"My film," he said. And I knew it was important to him because he couldn't quite look me in the eye.

I told myself I would not tease him. If it was bad I would let him down gently, like Mum does with the boys when we've run out of cherry yoghurt.

Keith started talking. "I had this idea, sort of based on the play we did in class in Year Seven – *The Tempest* – where this girl has grown up on an island and never seen the real world. Her dad is a magician, and a bit of a control freak to be honest, and there's spirits and stuff and a shipwreck."

I remembered doing that play. "Why did Miss Tunks give that big part to Shazna? She was so bad! I had to be the fairy thing, the spirit, Ariel. Sanjay and Ed called me 'TV' for weeks. That was *so* not fair."

"Seren, will you let me finish? Shazna is not going to be in my film, OK? And like I said, it's only *based* on *The Tempest*. And anyway, you being Ariel was the best thing about it." He flicked through the red notebook while he talked.

Keith thought I was good. I *was* good. Christina had said so at the time, even Miss Tunks.

I listened and said nothing for ages while Keith talked me through it. Downstairs, I heard the front door slam. It was Sasha, come in from work.

24

"I better go," Keith said, getting up. "You read through it and let me know what you think. Add some notes, anywhere you want. You've always got good ideas, Seren. See you tomorrow."

"Will do." I lowered my voice in case Sasha came up the stairs and I didn't hear. "You reckon Luke's in the shop for 11.30?"

Keith nodded.

"Then we'll be there at 11.20."

"Shall we synchronise our watches?"

"Do I look like James Bond?" I said.

Keith shrugged. "Well maybe not Daniel Craig, but sometimes, if it's a bit dark and you're frowning, you could pass as one of the old, craggy ones…"

"Keith!"

He ran out of the room before I could hit him with a pillow.

★★★

Keith's story wasn't bad at all. It wasn't a whole story, more like notes and sketches, and some of his drawings even made me laugh. It was about this girl who's lived all of her life on one estate, cut off from the world by a river and a motorway. It sounded a lot like where we lived. She was called Miranda, though, same as in the play. I liked that. Miranda. In Keith's notebook it was about Miranda wanting to see the world and being trapped on an estate.

There were spirits, but they weren't people dressed up as ghosts, they were in the place, in the buildings and in the new Light Railway. Anyway, at the end, the world comes to the girl, in the Olympics. I did think it was good, but I thought he could make it better.

☆☆☆

I was still sitting on my bed reading Keith's notebook when Sasha came in and changed out of her waitress's white shirt and black trousers.

"Your dad gave me an extra tenner this afternoon," Sasha said. She stood in front of the cupboard and swished through the clothes on her half of the rail. "I couldn't believe it, the place isn't exactly heaving with customers and your dad is usually so tight."

"He is not!" I said. Someone had to defend him.

Sasha shrugged. "Well, OK, *he's* not tight exactly but his mum, your Nene, oh my days, what a nightmare!"

I said nothing. I was not going to defend Nene. Nightmare was a totally fair description. Nene didn't like any of us, especially not Mum or me. Mum had explained it wasn't my fault, that Nene thought my dad had let himself down by falling in love with her.

Sasha went on, "She usually has her beady eye on him. Doesn't let any money out of her sight, that woman. I reckon something's up. He gave me one for you too. He seemed kinda odd."

I looked up. Sasha was holding out a tenner. "For me?"

Sasha nodded. "I know! It's not like him at all. Maybe he's ill. Anyway, this lovely tenner is going straight into my dress fund with my wages. I am going to have something so special for the end of term Prom..." She folded the money into her bank stuff and shut it in her drawer.

"Odd?" I said, sitting up. "You said my dad looked odd. What d'you mean?"

"Worried." Sasha turned towards me. "More worried than normal, you get me? And tired."

Now *I* was worried. Last time I'd seen him he'd been talking to Nene in Turkish a lot. I don't speak it at all, just hello, goodbye and counting to ten, but even so, I could tell there were problems.

Nene never let him forget how stupid he was to spend all that money on doing the whole place out like the inside of a cave, a few years ago. I couldn't bear it if they had to close. I knew how hard he'd worked.

"Yeah, OK. I'll get myself over there after school this week," I said. On the table by my bed was the blue glass eye pendant he'd given me when I was born. For good luck, to watch over me. I picked it up and turned it over and over in my hand.

"I hate that bloody thing!" Sasha said. She'd never liked it. "Can't you put it away? It really creeps me out."

I shoved it in the drawer with my knickers. "So, Sash, are you going out?" I said. Silly question.

"There's a party at this youth club over in Clapton."

"You're not staying over at Fay's though?" I said. I needed her back here, reasonably early, not looking completely washed-out. "Are you, have you, I mean you're not, you're not going out with someone, anyone... yet?"

"What are you on about?" Sasha looked at me as if I was more than one kind of nuts.

"You and Luke?"

Sasha flushed. "No! Anyway, it's none of your business." She turned away. It was like her face had one of those noisy metal shutters and it had just clanged down.

"Oh. Right. Sorry, Sash." I took a deep breath. "Are you busy, maybe? Tomorrow?"

Sasha looked at me. "Why?"

I had my reasons and everything rehearsed, and now I'd been reading Keith's stupid notebook all my thoughts had dribbled out of my head into thin air. "Tomorrow morning! Not too early, don't worry! It's a surprise. A surprise, that's it!"

"Well, keep your hair on, Seren. Maybe. I'll see." I knew that was a yes. Sasha turned back to the cupboard. "Have you seen my blue top? You haven't gone and borrowed it, have you?"

I had seen it. It was her favourite and she looked great in it. But I hadn't borrowed it. Not the way she meant, anyway.

"No." I flicked through Keith's notebook. "You know I can't wear your clothes." I gave her a wounded kind of look. Even though Sasha was older than me she was tiny and curvy and I was tall and straight-up-and-down. "Maybe it's in the wash," I said.

I really was getting better at lying. But she'd need to wear it tomorrow.

Sasha did a big, dramatic sigh and I felt a tiny bit

guilty. But it was for a good cause. I looked at the clock. I was so excited I would spill if I wasn't careful. This time tomorrow Sasha would be walking on air, and she'd have me to thank.

3

IN THE PARADISE INTERNATIONAL
FOOD AND WINE SUPERMARKET

I woke up thinking about Keith's shop. It was the biggest shop on the estate, bigger than the betting shop next door, with three aisles crammed with all sorts of stuff. If you wanted anything else (and Keith's shop did sell everything), you'd have to go to the brand-new, all-night express supermarket. They were building it on the road that would – once it had opened – lead on to the Olympic park. I'd told Keith's mum loads that even when it did open they should be all right, because no Tesco I'd ever seen sold crispy pork, or White Rabbit Chinese sweets.

I looked at the clock on the dressing table. It was only nine o'clock and my stomach was turning over and over like one of those gymnasts with sticky-out bunches that wins gold medals.

In her bed across the room, Sasha was still asleep. She made a whiffly noise and turned over as if she could hear me thinking, which, I told myself, was rubbish.

This will work, I said out loud but very quietly. Sasha would be thrilled, Fay would be awestruck and she would tell Christina and maybe things would change at school. Me and Keith might even get to be cool. Fingers crossed.

Under the pillow, my phone alarm went off on vibrate. I turned it off and flicked through my inbox. The last text I'd had was from Keith, yesterday morning. I scrolled down my contacts and before I let myself get really depressed at the shortness of the list I turned it off and sat up. I wasn't going to do that any more. I was someone new. My brother was singing at the Olympics, Sasha was about to have the best Leaving Prom ever, and Keith and me were going to make a brilliant film. Life was good.

Before I woke Sasha up, I put her blue top back in her drawer and made her and Mum a cup of tea.

The boys were watching cartoons, Denny had the remote and Arthur was whining, "Den-ny! Denny! I want to watch the o-ther siiiide…"

32

"Can't. I'm in charge." Denny waved the remote just out of Arthur's reach.

"Denny!" Arthur squealed, and jumped up and down, his face red with anger. "It's not fair! Denny, you are a slug-brain! A poo-head." Arthur turned his voice up to loud. "A MR STUPID POO-HEAD SLUG-BRAIN!"

Denny shouted back. "I'm gonna be the one *on* the telly and in the papers. People are gonna see me all over the world. You'll never get on the telly because you're a troll. A tiny troll-face boy. You'd only be on one of them shows, *The Troll-Face Boy of Hackney…*"

Arthur crumpled. "That's not true! Seren! Tell him that's not true!" Arthur looked at me, bottom lip stuck out a mile and wobbling like jelly.

"Denny!" I said.

Denny just sat there grinning, holding the remote. "Troll boy."

Arthur started punching him, and when that didn't work, lay back on the sofa and kicked him, his legs spiralling in the air like a toddler having a tantrum.

Denny just smiled, which made Arthur worse.

"Arthur. Stop it!" I pulled him away. His face was red and blotchy. "It's Mum's day off. Don't make her come down, not yet."

"I hate him!" Arthur said. "He said I was a troll!"

"Well, you are…" Denny said.

I took a deep breath. "No, Arthur. You are not a troll. Denny, apologise. Now! Or I'll take the remote upstairs with me."

"You're not the mum, you know," Denny said, scowling. "You're not even my sister, you're only my half-sister…"

For a second I didn't say anything. The words stung like a slap round the face.

"Denny!" I was shocked, and Denny realised what he'd said and went pale. Arthur smiled and said, "Ummm-mm" in that sing-song, little-kid way.

"Sorry, Seren," Denny said quickly, without being asked. "I am, Seren, really. I never meant…" He couldn't look me in the face.

"OK, done now," I said, and it came out flat and unwobbly, even though I thought I might be sick. "Say sorry to Arthur too, while you're at it."

"Sorry Arthur."

I was still moving in slow motion. Of course I was only his half-sister, that wasn't exactly breaking news. I told myself I was totally lucky it had taken him ten years to think of it.

I went into the kitchen and picked up the teacups.

We were not a family like you see on the telly. OK, maybe in one of the soaps where they're all complete nutters. Me and Sash have different dads and different last names. She's Sasha Campbell Brown, Brown for her dad who died before I was born. And me, I'm Seren Campbell Ali for my dad who runs the restaurant – Mum said it was true love for about a week. She also said he's a kind man, a too-soft-for-his-own-good man, and that's where I get it from, whatever 'it' is. The boys have the same dad, and I can remember him and the rows, so the boys are both just Campbell.

So we're all half-sisters and brothers. But like Mum says, we're not half a family, never just half a family. She won't have the word half in our house. She says it's the worst word in the world and we're not half of anything. We're whole, she says.

That's why it was such a shock. Denny had never thrown that at me. Not in all his ten years. Ever.

I took two cups of tea upstairs. Mum's door was propped open and she was sitting up in bed. I could see she was halfway through her brick of a book. I put the tea down on her bedside table.

"Thanks, love." She looked at me, and patted the bed next to her. So I put Sasha's tea down and slid into Mum's bed.

She put the book down, spread flat so as not to lose her place. "Are things OK?"

"Yeah," I said. "'Course." I put my head down on her shoulder, shut my eyes and breathed her in.

When Mum first started work driving the buses, I had this stupid idea that she would come home smelling of buses and not of Mum. You know that smell? That sort of sun-through-scratched-windows-and-old-chips-and-fizzy-drink kind of smell. She never did, obviously.

"Are you still checking I don't smell of bus?" she said.

I smiled.

"Everything's all right, isn't it?" Mum said. She smoothed the hair away from my forehead with her hand. "Oh, I wouldn't be your age again for any money," she said. "Thirteen!" There was a sort of sad laugh in her voice, like she was remembering.

I shut my eyes. It was lovely lying there, listening to her voice.

"You know you're really lucky, you are," Mum went on. "A gang of good friends, I mean, Christina's almost like another sister to you..."

I moved away and sat up. I didn't want to think about it and most of all I didn't want Mum worrying about something that had happened ages ago and was most definitely old news....

"It's all cool, Mum." I smiled and picked up Sasha's tea. "S'brilliant about Denny, isn't it?"

"Seren?" she said, and her voice sounded a little bit too sad for my liking.

"Mum, really. It's all good. Better than good. I'm making a film with Keith..."

"Keith? That's great!"

"I'm fine," I said, and smiled wide to prove it. Then I scurried out and was across the landing and back in our room before she could say anything else.

"Sasha. Sash!" I nudged my sister awake. "You promised."

"Promised what?" she mumbled.

"To get up, remember? I said it was a surprise. And look, remember that top you were on about? Well, clever Seren found it for you."

Sasha hugged me.

We got to the shop just in time. As we rounded the

corner I got a text from Keith. The *Paradise* has mirror glass windows so you can't see in.

L HERE, read the text. BUT OTHRS WTH HIM.

I put my arm through Sasha's.

"Is this the surprise?" she said, taking her sunglasses off.

"No, I just need something…"

Sasha's phone rang. I knew it was Fay because Sasha's got a special ringtone for her, that number one by the American girl singer, the one with the voice that does all those wobbly bits. Loud. Very loud. Sasha unhooked herself from me and answered.

"Gotta get this, Ser." Sasha had saved up for one of those new phones with touch screens and everything, and she loves it almost as much as she loves Luke Beckford.

Sasha was soon having an even louder conversation with Fay, while staring at herself in the mirror glass of the supermarket. I had to go in, and she had to come with me. I walked to the shop entrance. I could see Keith at the till, pointing round the corner to the cereal aisle. I really didn't want Sasha doing the girly phone thing in front of all those boys. Not cool.

I snuck in and saw Jamie Kendrick, who is six-foot-something and the school goalie, towering over the top of the aisle. He hadn't seen me. I could hear them chatting and laughing.

My mind was racing. It was going to be hard to get Luke to notice Sasha when he was with his mates. I listened. It sounded like four of them at least, and he was there, that was his voice, teasing someone about an easy goal.

I ran back outside. Sasha was twirling a ringlet of dark brown hair, watching herself in the mirror.

"Yes, Sasha," I said. "You are beautiful but will you come inside." And I did mean it. She was lovely, my sister, honey-brown skin, dark-brown hair that might just be black. Why couldn't Luke see how lucky he would be to have a girlfriend like her?

Sasha cupped her hand over the phone. "Can't I wait out here?"

"No! Finish your call! Please!"

"Seren, what is up with you?" She spoke to Fay again. "Excuse me, but my baby sister is giving me so much grief."

I winced at the word 'baby'. "Sasha, come on!"

Sasha covered the phone again and rolled her eyes. "What is your problem? I am coming, OK? Do I have to hold your hand to go shopping now?"

I sighed and went inside and hoped she'd follow.

The boys had moved to the chiller counter. It was easy to find them because one of them was laughing really loud. I kept my distance, just out of sight on the other side of the cleaning powder.

"You're never asking her?" That was Luke. His voice sounded really nasty. I could practically hear him making a screwed-up-in-disgust face.

Then I realised. They weren't talking about football any more. They were talking about girls. I felt my stomach do that super-speed swoop it only usually does in tower block lifts. Thirtieth floor to ground level in seconds.

They were saying things about some of the girls in Sasha's year. Horrible things. Talking about them like they were animals. No, worse than animals. Meat. Lumps of meat, like the cold, crispy pork and dead barbecue duck hung up on hooks by the checkout.

Ugly words. Horrible words. I couldn't believe that Luke, with his floppy hair and girl-magnet smile would say such disgusting things.

Then Sasha's name. He said Sasha's name and someone else laughed. I screwed my eyes up tight, willing them to stop, but it didn't work. I thought I was going to be sick. I could feel all the blood draining away from my face and rushing back to my heart.

At least Sasha wasn't hearing this.

Luke went on. "I asked her for this picture, yeah, for the Leavers' Book...."

I felt someone take hold of my hand and squeeze it. It was Sasha, she was standing right next to me and I realised I didn't know how long she'd been there.

"Sasha Campbell Brown?" one of them said, shaking his head. "She's so after you, Luke man, it is sad!"

Luke laughed. "Sasha? Fay's mate? That is one mad-looking girl... we got her down as Miss Desperate 2012! If there was a gold medal for stalking, she'd get it!" Luke laughed the loudest.

I saw Sasha's face begin to crumple. I was shaking my head.

"You're not, Sash, you're so not!" I said it too loud. Suddenly, there was Jamie Kendrick looking down at us from over the Persil Non Bio.

He coughed.

Sasha dabbed at the mascara from where it had started to run under her eyes. I could hear the blip of the till, but nothing else. It was perfectly quiet.

Sasha blinked. I picked up some washing powder. From the other side of the aisle I heard Luke saying, "What! What?"

Jamie looked at us. "Sasha," he said, and waved a silly little wave. "Hi."

Luke said, "Oops!" More laughter. Loads of laughter.

I looked back at Jamie. He looked embarrassed. The others didn't seem to care.

Sasha pulled away but I kept hold of her. "Let me go, Seren," Sasha said in a quiet, tiny-girl voice.

"No," I said, low. "Nobody talks to my sister like that." I thought I'd said it quietly but there was a chorus of 'ooohs' from the chiller-cabinet aisle.

I took a deep breath. I reminded myself that I had promised not to take any more snide remarks or giggles. I had promised that no one was going to make me or anyone I loved feel small and worthless ever again. I had made this mess. Now I was going to clean it up. I walked round to where the four boys in the football gear were still laughing. Well, all except Jamie.

Sasha let go of me and ran to the door. "Seren, come on!"

"No!" I faced the boys. They were just little boys, I said to myself. Like Denny and Arthur, only bigger and more stupid. One hundred million times more stupid. "Shame on you!" I tried to shout, but I could hear my voice was wobbly.

Luke Beckford had his hand over his mouth to cover his snaky, pretty-boy smirk.

"You!" I pointed at him with the box of washing powder, which was still in my hand. "Don't you ever," I was boiling over, "ever, talk about my sister like that!"

His stupid hair flopped into his stupid mouth.

This was the opposite of how it was supposed to happen. I wanted to make them hurt but they just laughed more. I wanted them to know how Sasha felt now.

"Sasha is lovely and you…" The words seemed to fall out of my mouth. "Mr Stupid Luke. You are a waste of space… a slug-brain!" I shut up. I was saying exactly what I was thinking. I slapped my hand over my mouth. I almost said poo-head. I wanted to say much, much worse.

Suddenly, there was Keith. He yanked me away and the washing powder jumped out of my hand and landed with a thump on the floor.

The box exploded in a cloud of blue-and-white, soapy snow.

43

Outside, Sasha was waiting round the corner, face to the wall, make-up smeared. "You bloody idiot, Seren!" She was sobbing, her face red and angry.

I put my hand out but she wrenched it away. I reached out again. but she slapped my hand away, hard.

"Ow! Sasha!" I said. "That hurt."

"Good!" Her voice was hard.

"It'll be OK, Sasha. I'm sorry, I never meant it to come out like that. I thought... I thought he'd be there on his own. I thought he'd see you in your blue top..."

"You idiot!" Sasha hissed. She looked at me, and if looks could kill I would have been dead three times over.

"Sash, I never meant..."

"Shut up. Don't even talk to me." Sasha spat the words out. She took a deep breath in and wiped the tears away from her face. She looked straight at me. "You have made the biggest fool out of me! My life is over! Don't you see that? It is over! And it's your fault!"

Sasha turned and flicked her shiny hair, and stormed off in the direction of Fay's.

4
CASTING

Sasha didn't come home for ages. She called Mum to say she'd be staying at Fay's till late and not to worry. I made pasta with sauce for the boys but I couldn't eat a thing. Mum was 'at a really good bit' in her book so she didn't come down either. I looked at the boys snarking at each other while they ate, and I wished I was ten like Denny, or five like Arthur, and nothing much mattered except who could shovel their spaghetti down the fastest.

I had to keep myself doing stuff to not think about what had happened. The sound of Luke Beckford's voice, Jamie Kendrick smiling stupidly with a stuck-on smile and, worst of all, Sasha shouting at me. I pushed my plate away.

She will come round, I told myself. I remembered last Christmas when she got this huge make-up kit and I accidently mashed up one of the brushes, and she managed to hold out not talking to me for two whole days. I knew this was worse. I must have sighed out loud, cos Denny spoke.

"Are you OK, Seren?" He looked at me. "I'm sorry about earlier," he said. "Honest. You cook good tea and you're not bad for a big sister, believe."

"Good," I said. I told myself to try and be nice, Denny was trying.

"You're not cross with me, Seren?" Denny said

"No," I said. I knew I sounded cross, I couldn't help it. My face was sort of fixed down. And all those things Sasha had said were just going round and round inside my head.

"You should eat some of this, it's love-erly." Arthur smiled and pushed the food through the gaps in his teeth.

"Oh, don't do that, Art," I said.

"Laugh then, Seren. That's what you're s'posed to do."

"I'll tell her a joke," Denny said. "It's really good, this one... there's this bear, see..."

"Denny, I'm not in the mood!" I sounded like Mum when she didn't have a book on the go. I couldn't help it.

The boys looked crushed and I thought it was better if I just got out of the way. I went upstairs and turned on the computer.

★★★

I hadn't been on the thing for weeks now. When we first got it, me and Sasha would fight over it. Like the boys and the TV remote. We had an hour each after school and that was it.

I'd stopped using it because you couldn't help seeing what the others were doing, Christina and Shaz and Ruby. And it all sounded so great and I wasn't part of it any more. Where they were meeting on the weekend, who did what, when.

Going on those sites and having no one to talk to and seeing who did was a bit like, well it was more than just turning the knife. It was like taking the knife out and then stabbing it into the wound again and again.

I took a deep breath while it started up. *Sashness*. That was her password, and if I didn't know it off by heart it came up in the little box when I typed the s. I looked at her page. Across the top of the page next to a picture of her and Fay in the false eyelashes it said *Sasha is seriously shamed*.

OK, fair enough. I scrolled down to look at her messages. None from Fay, obviously, cos she was there talking to her, but some from Toyin and Debra in her class. All along the lines of "Oh my days! I just heard what happened!"

She was getting enough sympathy. Perhaps it would be OK. No perhapses. I called Keith.

"It'll take time," he said. "You know that."

I went to bed early and pretended to be asleep when she came in. I lay there listening to her getting ready for bed, and I wanted so much to turn round and to talk to her. We were sisters, weren't we? I mean, I know we fall out and row sometimes but it's never for ever, is it?

When me and Sash were little we would reach out across the gap and hold hands.

I waited until she had flicked her bedside light out, then I turned over to face her. She was turned away from me in a ball. I knew she couldn't be asleep. Not really. I watched her back. I could tell she wasn't asleep. I coughed. A little 'I'm not asleep either' cough. So she'd know.

Nothing.

I saw the numbers on the alarm clock flip over five more minutes and I coughed again. A quiet cough.

"Seren, I know you're awake." Sasha didn't turn round. "And I hope you feel like shit, because I do."

"Sasha, I am *so* sorry," I said.

"From now on things will be different," she said. She still didn't look at me.

"Yes, I know. I'll be..."

"Listen!" she said, and I heard the hardness in her voice. "After today, after this, now. I am not talking to you. I am not talking to you and I don't want you to talk to me again. Ever."

"What?" I sat up.

She didn't move. "You heard me. Not at school, not at home. Just leave me alone."

"Sasha?"

She didn't reply.

"OK, school," I said. There'd been whole weeks when Sasha had decided she wouldn't talk to me at school, that was almost normal. "But home? We have to share a room," I said. "You're my sister," I said. I was sounding a bit wobbly, I could hear it in my voice.

Sasha said nothing.

It took me ages to get to sleep.

Sasha didn't talk to me while she got dressed, and she never said a word at breakfast. Although Sasha doesn't really eat breakfast, she just takes a bit of toast as she walks out. Mum didn't notice, not because of her book, but because she was on *earlies*, so I dropped the boys at their school, and walked in with Keith.

"Things still bad?" Keith said. It must have been all over my face.

"Whatever you do, Keith," I said, "never get all..." I couldn't think of the word.

"All what?" he asked.

"All *I'm never speaking to you ever again*," I said.

"Oh, that." Keith waved a hand. "I reckon people watch too many soaps. My mum watches them all the time, and even she thinks they're mad. People are so fickle."

"Fickle?" I said. "What does fickle mean?"

"Like changing their minds all the time. You know. In those shows they love someone for ever and then fifteen minutes later they've forgotten whoever it was who was their absolute and total soulmate, and they've decided to bury him alive and have fallen in love with the doctor."

I smiled. "It was stupid though, wasn't it, what I did? *Gauche*. Miss Tunks was right, wasn't she?"

Keith shrugged. "Bad luck too. But look on the positive side. At least you know Luke is a complete... what did you say? *Slug-brain*, I think it was..."

"Keith!" I swung my bag at him. "You know, I nearly called him a poo-head too."

"Poo-head?" Keith stroked an imaginary beard. "I think poo-head fits the boy rather well."

I smiled. He was right. I wouldn't want that toe-rag going out with Sasha in a million million years. Maybe one day she'd thank me. One day when we were old and grey....

"Anyway," Keith went on, "who'd have guessed it would have ended up so soapy in more ways than one. After you dropped that box of Persil I was cleaning it off the floor all day. Came up super-clean though. Actually came up rather too clean. That Mrs Arnold from the flats nearly fell over on it. She could have sued me, she said."

"The soap powder!" I hit my own forehead in what I hoped was a Homer-style facepalm. "I should've helped."

"You should've." Keith nodded. "But because I am nice I am going to let you off with coming filming this week after school."

"Yes. Anything. I will do anything, Keith."

"Well there's a couple of things I need to ask you about."

"Go on then," I said. The bell went off for lessons and everyone got up.

"Well, first of all I'd like to ask your dad about his restaurant…"

"Yeah! It's perfect! Just right for the scene in the middle! I had exactly the same idea! He won't mind. Of course I'll ask him."

Keith never got round to asking about the second thing because we spent the rest of the walk talking about how Dad's restaurant would make a brilliant cave-like set, and I said I thought my Nene would make an excellent Caliban without any make-up or special effects.

I don't know what I was expecting in school. Mondays we always have Form Time and I was sitting with Keith. He was chatting about his film when they came in. I suppose it's hard not to have a sixth sense about people talking about you, or laughing about you more like, but Christina makes it easy.

She and Shazna were just standing there in the doorway, looking at me and laughing. Their hands were up in front of their mouths, trying to hide what they were doing. Just like babies who think you can't see them when they've got their hands over their eyes. Then I thought, well, maybe they want me to see what they're doing. They want me to know how stupid I am. I turned away.

They all floated into class. Ruby was with them now, looking at me like I was the lowest form of life, something that hadn't even evolved. Christina was loud now, to Ruby, so everyone would hear. "Did you hear what Seren did over the weekend? I feel so sorry for poor Sasha."

"Yeah, well, what do you expect from Seren? She's like – like a giant idiot."

I winced. If there had been any chance of some kind of, not truce exactly, not me and Christina being best mates again, just being any kind of mates – then that was over. I was sort of surprised that it still hurt.

I wanted to say something back, but I had done the standing-up-for-myself thing, and look where that had got me. I bit my lip and looked away.

Keith stopped talking, looked at me, then at them.

"Breathe slowly, deeply and slowly," he hissed. "It'll make the redness go away."

"Oh God, I'm not going red, am I?"

"At least you know *why* they're looking at you," he said.

"And everyone else will know why too!"

"Seren, allow it. You can't let it get to you. They'll just be worse if they think you care."

He was right of course.

"Anyway, *giant idiot*'s not so bad as far as insults go. Try and think about something else," Keith said. "Think about the film, think about that IT homework I bet you never did, and how you're gonna have to ask to copy mine."

The rest of the morning was the same. Christina and her lot doing the wind-up thing, talking about how she would never humiliate her big sister, ever. Then me almost going off, and Keith calming me down.

By lunchtime, I thought I had got through the worst. I had worried that Luke Beckford and his lot would give me a load of trouble. But they didn't seem to care or notice. I was just some Year Eight girl like hundreds of others. It was a relief to be a nobody. But I had forgotten Sasha and Fay in the dinner hall, giving out dirty looks like Jehovah's Witnesses give out leaflets.

Keith and me went outside.

"So I see it like a story, obviously. About this girl who's never been out of her estate, who doesn't realise there's this whole world just on her doorstep." Keith was talking about his film. "But, it's like every shot is gonna be really beautiful too."

We were sitting on the old metal bench by the chain-link fence. It was OK at either end but the middle was battered and slightly warped where someone had tried to make a fire underneath it.

Suddenly I realised we had company. I sat up and nudged Keith.

It was Christina and Shazna.

"Lost Ruby?" I said, and wished I sounded less snarky and more cool. Snarky showed I cared.

"We want to talk to Keith," Christina said, not even looking at me. This girl had been my best friend for years. I couldn't count the number of sleepovers I had spent in her room, or even the times I'd been to her nan's house in St Alban's.

I looked away. Took a deep breath. All last term they'd hated me for being mates with Keith. Now they wanted to talk to him.

Keith took a spring roll out of his plastic lunchbox. "So?" he said.

The girls flicked a look at me. Keith shrugged.

Christina sighed a big overdone sigh and crossed her arms. "Look," she said. "Miss Tunks says you're making a film. For that competition?"

"Yup," Keith said, dabbing a bit of food away from the side of his mouth. Keith is not like some boys who think that shovelling and eating are the same thing.

"She says," Christina said, "Miss Tunks thinks, you'll need help and that, and me and Shaz, well..."

Keith shook his head. "No, really, thanks, but no thanks." He smiled quickly and took a glug from his water bottle. He looked at me. I wondered if he was thinking about the time Christina called him a loser.

Christina folded her arms. "Keith, Miss Tunks thinks you're good." There was an edge to her voice. "I mean, everyone knows you know everything about films. And she's seen your idea."

I looked at Keith, I couldn't keep it in. "She has?" I said.

Christina smirked an *I know something you don't* smirk, and exchanged looks with Shazna.

Keith was cool. "Thank you, Christina. That's very kind of you to say." He closed his lunch box and put it back in his bag. Didn't look at them, took another drink from his water bottle.

"Keith! Do I have to spell it out?" Christina said.

"You're gonna need help. Actresses? Me and Shaz?" They both nodded. They looked at him and then at each other and then back to Keith.

"Yeah," Shazna said. "Miss Tunks said, it was sort of like *The Tempest* and that? And I was Miranda and everything that one time, so I pretty much know the part inside-out already."

Keith did up the cap on his water bottle slowly and calmly. He wiped his mouth with the back of his hand. He took a paper hanky from his bag and wiped his hands. Then he looked up at them.

"I think, girls, that might be a matter of opinion. And as I'm the director, you'll find that I make the decisions. So, thanks, but no thanks."

The girls made furious, huffy noises but didn't go away.

"But I can do it, Keith." Shazna sounded almost desperate.

"Sorry."

The girls looked at Keith, utterly gobsmacked that anyone would ever say no to them.

"Actually, wait," Keith said. "I'm not sorry. Remember last term?"

I flushed, remembering last term, and Christina did too, bright red. She opened and closed her mouth.

"I don't know why you two would want to have anything to do with me," Keith said coolly. "I certainly don't want either of you in my film."

Christina glared at us. "It'll be rubbish anyway." She looked back at Keith. "With her." She pointed at me. "You know it. You two are pond life."

Shazna tried her hardest at an evil look, but half her face seemed sort of frozen. I had to try hard not to laugh.

"Yeah," Shazna said. They linked arms and stalked off.

Keith took another swig of water, cool as anything.

"What did they think? That you'd be so honoured by their offer you'd be grateful?"

"Who knows?" Keith shrugged. "I wouldn't have those two anywhere near a film of mine. They are bitchy and vindictive."

"Good word. Vindictive." I nodded.

"And what's worse," Keith went on, lowering his voice as if Christina could hear round corners, "is that thing she does with her hands when she's on stage, no, scratch that, she does it in Drama too, when she's acting."

"I thought it was only me who noticed that!" I said. "It does my head in! She holds her hands flat at her

58

sides like paddles, or like those plastic doll's hands where the fingers are all stuck together."

"I know. It makes her look as if she's made of wood," Keith said. "And if those two think I had forgotten how they treated us both, they must be mad..."

I watched Christina and Shazna disappear inside the school. I was a bit surprised how good it felt. My KitKat tasted even more chocolatey and delicious than usual.

"So," Keith said, "I want to get it all shot as soon as possible. The closing date's in a month and I'm going to need all the editing time I can get."

"You never told me Miss Tunks had seen your idea!" I said.

"You don't like Miss Tunks."

"She doesn't like me."

"I've said it before, that is *so* not true."

"So who are you going to use in the film then, as the Miranda girl?"

"Well, it's not exactly Miranda," Keith said. "It's more like a character that's sort of inspired by Miranda, grown out of Miranda, not an exact copy just taken straight from *The Tempest* and stuck in 21st century London."

"I know all that!" I said. "I did read it. So who's it going to be? You can tell me, you know."

From across the other side of the grey tarmac playground the bell whirred for afternoon registration.

"Well, I was going to talk to you about this..." Keith said, getting up.

"So talk now. Tell me it's not Justine in the other class, or that Tasmin-who-thinks-she-knows-everything, please!"

"Justine?" Keith screwed up his face at the idea. "Give me some credit!" Keith pushed his glasses back up his nose. "Look, Seren, I was worried you'd say no, you've been in a bit of a bad way with all this stuff, with Sasha and that. But I was always going to ask you."

"Me? You want me to be in it?" I felt suddenly very excited and happy. "I mean, I know we're mates and that, Keith, but this is not just to make me feel better, is it? Cos that would be a mistake, obviously, and it's not just cos you want to film in my dad's place? Cos you know I would help out, Keith, even if I wasn't..." I was gabbling.

"Seren! Listen! No. It's none of that." Keith rolled his eyes. "I'm asking you because you would be best.

You're my mate and I can talk to you, sure, and that helps. But also you're really good at acting." He took a deep breath. "Now, are you coming to English or are you planning on being late?"

5
THE KUTEST KIDDIE

It was after school. Keith had gone to talk to Miss Tunks about cameras, and I thought he would be better off going on his own. I was off to Dad's to ask about the café, and still walking on air because I was going to be Miranda. I promised myself I would make Keith really proud.

Dad's place wasn't just any café. He always told people it was a bistro, or a restaurant. I thought restaurant was pushing it a bit myself, but seeing as I'd only ever been to Maccy D's, the bakers by the station, and a caff round the corner from Christina's Nan's in St Albans, I didn't really know. But restaurants on the telly always had candles and those enormous pepper grinders and Dad's place didn't.

Dad's place was proper Turkish like him, and he did really good *shish* and *lamacun* (say it lamajzhoon) which is like pizza. He'd also had the inside of it done up like a cave with grey-painted, pretend stone walls. It looked mad, believe. Anyway, that's why Keith wanted to film some of his film in there, because it was totally bonkers and not like any place that exists in real life.

So I waited at the bus stop, thinking about all this. It was on Mum's route and I was sort of hoping it would be Mum's bus. We always had a little chat when she was driving along. It made me feel proud, standing up there near the driver's bit. Plus it was the one time you could be sure she wasn't stuck into a book. She had to be in the real world, looking for little kids who just might run into the road, stopping the bus early if there was an old lady who'd not quite made it to the stop.

But it wasn't Mum who came along, it was her mate Carol. "Hiya love, you up the High Street to your dad's?"

I said "yeah", swiped my oyster card, and sat down near the front.

Mrs Gold, one of Mum's regulars, got on and sat down in one of the priority seats for old people and pregnant women. Mrs Gold smiled at me and asked after Mum. Then her mate, Mrs Morris, got on and

Mrs Gold started chatting with her, which to be honest, was a bit of a relief.

I put my earphones back in, but even with my music playing I could hear them laughing and giggling like fifteen-year-olds.

I loved these buses, these little buses that went anywhere – not like the double-deckers. These buses, Mum's buses, went through all the back streets, criss-crossing the estates. Once I'd got over the stupid idea of Mum smelling of bus, I was really proud. I would wave at her when she went past. Most of the time she was concentrating really hard so she never saw me, but I would always point her out. *There's my mum.* I stopped doing that when Christina said it was stupid, she was *only* a bus driver.

I shuddered, remembering. Mum always said no one was ever *only* anything.

On the empty seat next to me was the local paper, folded up so you could only read half the headline: *Olympics.* All the headlines round here had been Olympic this or that for so long it felt funny thinking the Games were actually going to happen.

I shook the paper out and flipped past the latest stories of jackings, school plays, and celebrities opening shopping centres. The only decent thing about our local paper was the problem page, but this week even the problems weren't as problemy as my life. Not a patch on it: *Girl, 13, shunned by sister even though she was trying to do something good.*

I turned another page. *School Singing Stars Chosen for Olympics.* There was Denny's choir with Denny beaming out from the middle of the photo. Mum would be over the moon.

I took out the page and folded it carefully so the picture was in the middle. They'd even spelt his name right underneath, *Denzel Campbell, age 10*, and he didn't look too bad, not like the big-headed, little brother, wind-up machine he could be in real life. I smiled back at the picture before putting the page into my bag. Denny would have it framed, and Mum would tape it up on the flip-down mirror in the front of her bus, next to the one of Arthur dressed up as the Gruffalo when they had Book Week at his nursery last year.

I turned the rest of the paper over. *Kutest Kiddie Kontest*, it said. Underneath the headline were twenty or so square portraits of kids, some babies but some as old as nine. *Keep those entries flooding in*, it read. *Local photographer in Kingsland Centre this weekend, all welcome!* If Arthur wanted to get his picture in the paper, maybe there was something I could do about it.

"High Street!" the bus driver called out. I'd been so busy I hadn't noticed we'd arrived.

"Thanks, Carol." I always say thank you to bus drivers, it makes them happy.

★★★

The Cave was empty. Mehmet, Dad's cousin, who's around twenty and head waiter, was having a cig on the pavement outside.

"Haven't you got tables to wait on, then?" I said.

"Place is emptier than Tesco's car park at midnight. S'been like this for nearly a month now," Mehmet said and blew out a big, blue cloud of smoke. Sasha used to have a sort of crush on him until she smelt those cigarettes. "I don't know how long..." Mehmet stopped mid-sentence and threw his half-smoked cig into the gutter.

I looked to see what had made him jump. I should have known. It was Nene. I tried not to smile. I was glad it wasn't just me who was scared of her. Dressed head to foot in black, she launched into a verbal attack on Mehmet, full volume, non-stop Turkish. I couldn't catch a word of it, but her size, short and square, and her face and tone, made her seem more like one of those vicious little Staffordshire bull terriers than a little old lady. I stepped back. She stopped, looked me up and down like I was lower than dirt, and went inside.

"Hello, Nene," I called after her. She didn't bother to look round and, to tell the truth, I'd probably have fallen over if Nene even tried to be nice to me.

Mehmet looked at me, shrugged, and scurried in after her.

Nene is my grandmother. Now I know grannies are supposed to be all loved-up over their grandchildren, but it was never like that with me and Nene. Mum said not to worry, Nene was like that with everyone, but I knew she held a special place in her heart for hating me. I was proof that, in Nene's eyes, her lovely son was once, long ago, less than perfect.

Inside the Stone Cave, Dad was sitting at a table near the back, tapping away at a laptop.

I smiled and waved, but it was obvious I wasn't going to get as much as five minutes out of Dad with Nene there, jabbing her finger at him like a demented troll. Maybe this was her cave and Dad had fixed it up so she'd feel right at home. The walls were all grey and had been plastered by Dad and his mates so that they looked like rock rather than walls.... But rock that had been painted Dulux Elephant Grey rather than any real-life cave I ever saw.

Today the restaurant was very empty.

"Mehmet," I said, "is it like this in here all the time?" Mehmet was hard at work, wiping a table which looked perfectly clean already.

"Mondays, yes. Tuesdays too. Thursdays sometimes your dad's mates come in after work, and Fridays and Saturdays... well, it's not much better." He leant close. His breath really was smoke-fuelled toxic. "But things are bad." He lowered his voice."I don't know if you know all this, but Nene wants him to sell up. She wants to go home."

"Home?" I said. "Wood Green?"

"No, Seren, Cyprus!"

"Sounds all right to me," I said. "Better than all right in fact. Maybe Dad'd get more customers in here if Nene wasn't lurking in corners, snarling."

Mehmet almost laughed. "No, Seren, you don't get it. Nene wants everyone to move with her, your dad and Sherifa and the girls, my Mum and Dad."

"What!" I was shocked now. "Dad's going to Cyprus?"

"It's not definite. And I am going nowhere. I am

totally staying in London! There's nothing to do over there at all."

"I wouldn't know," I said. Dad had taken me once when I was tiny, before him and Sherifa had had their kids, but I could hardly remember it at all.

"I don't want to be out of a job," Mehmet said. "Your dad says he's waiting for the Olympics. Holding out till then. Says there'll be so much trade, but Nene, she doesn't believe him. She says her heart will give out if they stay in Dalston a month longer."

"So we need more trade or she'll get her way?" I said.

"Exactly."

We both looked at Nene. I heard the word 'Olympics' and the word 'heart-attack'. So maybe those words don't really translate into Turkish. I thought that there was nothing that would stop Nene. Even if she had a heart attack she had so much energy she would still keep going. Actually I would have put good money on Nene not having a heart at all.

Dad looked like a beaten man. I felt a wave of 'sorry' coming off him towards me, and I looked back at him with what I hoped was my sympathetic face. He smiled at me over Nene's shoulder. I made a phone shape with my hand and mouthed, 'I'll call.'

Nene saw me looking, and gave me a dirty look so filthy I could have used it to grow vegetables.

"She still hates you more than me, then?" Mehmet whispered.

"Oh yes," I whispered back. "I am top of Nene's most hated. I doubt if there is anything you could do to take my crown," I said, and walked out.

This was not actually true. I think Nene hates my mum a sliver more than me, but as she never has to see Mum, I get it all because I am walking, breathing proof that once Dad fell in love and had a kid with someone who was not Turkish. Dad has told me over and over to take no notice, and I do try my best.

I had only got as far as the cinema when I heard Dad shouting behind me. "Seren! Babe!"

I turned round and he caught up with me, out of breath from running.

"Are you OK?" he said. "Nene! I know! I'm sorry, love! You know what she's like." He hugged me tight. "Seren. I don't see you enough. You should come round to the house. Sherifa loves you too, you know that."

Sherifa is Dad's wife.

"Sherifa's cool," I said. It's true, we get on, she is lovely. "But what about Nene?"

Dad made a face. "Maybe not the house then." Nene lives with Dad. "Come to the Cave on Wednesday. At least that way you'll miss Nene, she'll be taking the girls to their music class." The girls are my other sisters, Gamze and Ayshe. They're OK too. I even quite like helping with them sometimes, in the summer.

"Are you all right, Dad? The business?" I said. "Only Mehmet said... he said you might be moving."

"Where d'you get that idea from?" he said. But he wasn't looking me in the face. "It's all fine, Seren."

Why did I not believe him?

"I got the tenner. From Sasha last Saturday."

"Yeah, I thought it might be the last bit of money you see from me for the time being. Tell Sasha I'll be sad to lose her." He shrugged. "But I can't afford another pair of hands. There isn't the trade."

"Hang on." I was still processing what Dad had just said. "You mean she's fired?"

"I'm not Alan Sugar, babe. I just can't keep her on any more. I can't afford it."

I folded my arms. "Did you tell her all this? On Saturday?"

Dad said nothing.

"Oh, Dad! You didn't, did you?"

"Not out like that. I couldn't, I mean I know how much the job means to her. To your mother."

"You should have told her, Dad! She's saving up for her big Prom dress and everything!"

"I was going to call," he said, not looking at me. "You can tell her for me, yeah?"

"Dad!"

"So, I'll see you Wednesday, love," he said and kissed me on the cheek. "I better get back."

"Nene?" I said, crossing my arns. I wanted to say "Why are you going, why won't you talk to me?" But I couldn't.

Dad nodded. "Nene."

I watched him go. He seemed a lot older than Mum. Maybe he should read some books. It seemed to work for her. I hadn't even told him about Keith and the film, but I figured that Dad owed me that much. I texted Keith on the way to the bus stop to say that that we were on for Wednesday, and tried not to think about Cyprus.

I stood at the bus stop outside the cinema, trying to think of an easy way to tell Sasha, who is not even talking to me, that she is out of a job. The bus came far too quickly for my liking.

When I looked in my bag for my Oyster Card I saw

the newspaper picture of Denny, and remembered the *Kutest Kiddie Kontest* for Arthur. Denny would have his singing, I'd be in Keith's film and Arthur could be Kute. I sighed. That just left Sasha. No date for the Prom, public humiliation in her local corner shop and now no job. It just got worse and worse. Dad could be such an idiot sometimes!

Maybe that's where I got it from.

As the bus pulled away, the doors of the Rio cinema opened and dozens of women with pushchairs spilled out into the street. One chased after the bus and the driver waited for her and let her on.

"You saved my life!" The woman said to the driver. She was out of breath and pink in the face. "Thank you so much!"

"What is going on in that place now?" the driver said. "A mother's meeting?"

"No." The woman was still a bit out of breath. "It's mother and baby films. It's great!"

"What, like *Finding Nemo* or *Toy Story* or something?" asked the driver.

"No, *Kill Bill*," the woman said and went to sit down. The bus driver's face was a picture.

I knew what she meant. They had a mother-and-baby screening, where mums could come and bring their tiny babies, and they could just feed them or hold them while they watched a film.

The bus stopped at the lights, and suddenly I had an idea. I thought that Dad could do a special for the mums and babies.

What if Dad laid on tea and cake, and someone like me or Sasha – not Nene – could keep an eye on the babies while they chat? I happened to know, from years of research of course, that the only thing mums like more than cake is chat. Maybe that would help. Keith knew everyone at the cinema by their first name, he was bound to have a number I could pass on. Dad could talk to them, or I could ask at Film Club. It was worth a try.

The bus swished past the shopping centre, where there was a brand new banner flapping in the wind: LONDON 2012 WELCOMES THE WORLD! it said.

Now I had more bad news. I sighed, so the glass of the window fogged up in front of my mouth. I didn't care about the world, I just wanted Sasha to welcome me. How was I going to manage that?

6
LIGHTS! CAMERA! ACTION!

"Once I've signed this out for you, Keith, this camera becomes your responsibilty, for the whole week," Miss Tunks said.

It was lunchtime, and me and Keith were in the Drama office. I was furthest away from the desk, backed into a shelf of multiple copies of *A Midsummer Night's Dream*.

"Yes, Miss Tunks." Keith nodded and cradled the camera in his hand as if it was a silver, metallic kitten. I wouldn't have been surprised if it had started purring.

"You know how it all works?" she said.

"Yes, Miss Tunks."

"And you'll be using your own memory stick?"

"Yes, Miss Tunks." Keith flicked the camera on and flipped out the viewing screen.

I had to admit it did look dinky and flashy and very, very lush.

Miss Tunks must have seen the look on my face. "And as it's signed out in your name, Keith, that means *you* will be the one using it and carrying it at all times."

"Yes, Miss Tunks."

"And not any persons round here with a talent for falling over..." She looked straight at me and I looked away. That woman would never let me forget the Christmas show.

"Right." Miss Tunks picked up the mug from her desk and took a sip. It read STAR in red letters. "I'll give you the key for the costume cupboard, Keith, make sure you lock up and give it back to me after lessons. I'll be in the staffroom. I'm sure it'll go well. You've got a great eye, don't forget that."

"No, Miss Tunks," Keith said, smiling, and she shooed us out.

Out in the corridor I mimicked, "No, Miss Tunks!" over and over until Keith had to push me to make me shut up.

"That is so why she likes you!" I said. "Three bags full, Miss Tunks..."

"Yeah. But I got the camera, didn't I?" He patted

his bag. "And I got the key to the costume cupboard." He twirled the key on its fat, plastic key-fob.

On the other side of the corridor, I saw Fay and some of Sasha's mates. They looked knives at me, but since they'd been doing that for the past three days it was starting to feel like normal.

"Have you told Sasha about her job yet?" Keith asked.

"Sort of," I said. "It's hard when she's not talking to me. At all."

"Seren!" Keith sighed. "You really don't do yourself any favours. The quicker it's done..."

"I wrote her a note," I said.

Keith looked at me and his face told me I was the biggest idiot in the whole school.

"There was nothing else I could do! She's never in the same space as me for more than a few seconds and if I so much as try to talk to her she looks away, moves away."

"You should have got your dad to do it."

"I wish! He's too much of a soft touch. That's his whole problem." I thought of Nene. "I was going to text her but that seemed a bit harsh. So I wrote her a note. I stuck it in her locker this morning. I expect she's read it by now."

I could still feel the Year Elevens staring as Keith opened the door to the costume cupboard, which was under the main stairs and next to the stage. It was bigger than an actual cupboard but not much, and it stank of old sweat and stale make-up. On either side were metal clothes-rails thick with floor-length dresses, cloaks and funny trousers, and on the floor were black bin-liners, marked with labels written in fat marker on sticky tape. One read TOGAS, another, OLIVER.

Me and Keith each took a rail, and started to look through it. Sometimes a heavy waft of stale sweat and old deodorant seemed to puff out of the clothes as if they were alive. "This is rank," I said, passing a mothy old velvet doublet and moving on past a Victorian crinoline, made out of what looked like net curtains. "You have to admit it does stink like someone's old armpits in here."

Keith breathed huffily. "We need to find something for Miranda."

"But you said earlier you wanted your Miranda to look ordinary," I said. I pulled out a Medieval dress complete with pointy hat and veil. "Like this, maybe?"

Keith rolled his eyes. "No! More ordinary, well, not

completely ordinary, out of the ordinary. You've got to stand out. You're not going to be saying anything so you've got to look different, exceptional...."

"Yeah, and not like some Turkish-English giant girl who likes her cake."

"You are so not fat!" Keith snapped. "Girls!" He pushed his glasses back up his nose. "It's because you are tall that you can wear anything," he said.

"Who are you all of a sudden? Gok Wan?"

"Seren!"

"Sorry." Christina had used that one on him so often it had got very stale.

"There's nothing here!" Keith leant against the wall and crossed his arms.

"We'll find something," I said.

"Miranda is supposed to be this girl who is trapped..." Keith sighed.

I opened a bag that said BUGSY MALONE. There was a twenties flapper dress which was cream-coloured and fringy. Shazna had worn something like it for the Christmas show, and I remembered being dead jealous. I looked at the flapper dress. Shazna's had been much prettier, more delicate. I closed the BUGSY MALONE bag and rummaged through the other black bin-liners: LEOTARDS, PANTOMIME

HORSE. Suddenly, there it was. GROVE END'S GOT TALENT. That was it, last Christmas. I pulled the bag open and looked inside. There was the mermaid's tail some girl in Year Nine had worn, a cat mask and a Superman outfit. I dug down deeper, touched something silky near the bottom and pulled.

There was the dress. I looked at it for a long minute, remembering the rehearsals we'd had all through November, me, Christina and Shazna. I thought it would be just me and Christina at first, but ever since the start of the autumn term things had been different. It hadn't been me and Chris any more, she hadn't been Chris any more. She had become Christina and it was always three of us, Shazna was always there.

Shazna hated Keith, she said he was a total weirdo just because he was a boy who talked to girls. I should have realised then just how bad things were. I still thought we could all be mates.

I even smiled, thinking about the time I suggested Shazna take the lead in the dance routine we'd worked out, watching her and Christina, and gradually realising, as December rolled round, that they didn't want me in it at all. Why didn't I take the hint? I shivered and closed my eyes. Because I had done all the work, sorted out the moves – everything.

I remembered standing on our school stage, looking like some kind of giant next to Shazna and Christina, grinning like an idiot, so happy to be up on stage. So excited to be there in the dark of the hall, the curtains pulled tight so the afternoon light wouldn't sneak through. There was a sudden rushing in my ears and I thought I would be sick if I remembered any more.

I snapped my eyes open and looked at the dress. I took deep breaths to make the vomity feeling go away, and forced myself to concentrate on here and now.

The dress was pale grey with silver sequins and fringing, that moved and rippled like water. I had wanted to wear this so much. Shazna got it because she was smaller than me, and to be honest it wasn't long enough to be a dress on me. I took my school jumper off and put the dress on over my shirt and school trousers. It was more of a tunic top on me. "What d'you think?" I said.

Keith got out the camera and flipped down the viewing screen. I pulled my best Kate Moss faces at him.

Keith looked at me seriously. He nodded his head. "You know what, Seren, maybe that's it...." He looked back at the flipped-down screen and smiled.

There was a high-pitched bleeping noise from the camera. "Dammit!"

"What's happened?"

"Dunno. I'll just pop back and see if I can find Miss Tunks. I won't be a sec."

After Keith had gone, I found a mirror behind one of the clothes rails and admired myself a bit. I did love this dress. I was mid-admire when the door flew open.

"Did she sort it?" I said, looking round.

But it wasn't Keith.

Standing in the open doorway was Sasha. For a tiny nano-second I thought she had come to find me to make everything up. We would be friends again. Or if not friends, then sisters.

"Fay said you were sneaking around in here." The tone of her voice made it obvious I had been wrong. And she wasn't alone. I could see Fay behind her, smiling.

"I'm not sneaking," I said. I stood up. The fringes of the dress rustled. Fay sniggered and I realised it wasn't just Sasha and Fay. There were others too, at least three or four.

One of them said, "What is she wearing?" And

I backed away into the dark. Sasha stepped forward into the cupboard, and even though my instinct was to shrink back I still couldn't prevent the tiny seed of happiness I felt because Sasha had come and found me.

She took a crumpled piece of paper out of her bag. It was my letter. She had read it! She must understand now, mustn't she? I had written that Dad told me he'd had to let her go, that he didn't want to and that he was really sorry. That the café wasn't doing too well and it wasn't anything she'd done.

"I'm really sorry," I said. "About the job."

I realised Sasha was red in the face. The corners of her mouth were pulled down into a frown. There was practically steam coming out of her ears. The tiny speck of happiness fizzled away into nothing. Sasha was so angry she might explode.

"You!" She waved the letter at me. "You did this! I bet you did."

I didn't get it. "Yes, I wrote it." I said. "Dad was such a chicken he couldn't get the words out, well, you know what he's like.... Can we talk about this at home, Sash, you know, there's loads of people...." I was gabbling. Trying to calm things down, but I could feel my heartbeat racing away.

"You wish!" Fay said.

"I bet," Sasha snarled. She took a deep breath. "I bet you put your dad up to this. I bet it was you who got him to sack me!"

"She must have," Fay said. "S'obvious."

"No, I never!" I was pleading. "Sash, I didn't!"

"I bet you went round there and told him to sack me! Are you doing my job now? Earning my money?"

I shook my head desperately. "No!"

"Well, you can tell him from me it was a stupid bloody job! A stupid bloody job!"

"It wasn't me, Sash! I would never do that! I wouldn't. Dad's losing money! He might have to shut down and move! It's not just about you!" I sighed. "He can't afford..."

"Don't give me that! Why did he give us that money? You know what? You don't know how much I hate that you're my sister!"

"Sasha?" I said. She was leaning towards me and I could feel the flecks of spit firing into my face.

Sasha's face had contorted. She looked like one of those stone things in old churches, all twisted up and almost crazy. "You screw up my social life! Did you know the whole year is laughing at me now? Did you? Every day in school the whole year is laughing at me."

"I never meant..."

"Shut up! And now this! Now my job!" She came closer so her head was almost touching mine and the door flapped shut. It felt as if I was trapped.

I was on the floor now, sitting on one of the bin-liners with Sasha shouting down at me, pointing her finger in my face, the hate streaming out of her. I turned away, I couldn't look into her eyes any more. I wanted the costume cupboard to swallow me up into its smelly darkness.

"You are evil and clumsy and stupid, and no wonder you have no friends except for that weirdo from the Chinese Supermarket. Nobody likes you, Seren. Have you got that? Nobody in this whole school!"

I didn't really see Sasha and Fay go because my eyes were all blurry, and it wasn't until Keith came back and passed me a bit of old Toga to blow my nose on, that I realised I was crying.

7

ONCE MORE, WITH FEELING

"You sure you're OK with this, love?" Mum said to me. Then she shouted after the boys. "Be good for your sister. If you muck around I'll know!"

But they had already jumped off the bus and Denny had started running hell-for-leather down the road.

"Seren!" Arthur said, holding out his hand for mine. "We're late."

"I'm coming."

"You are a star, you know that," Mum said. "I know you've been a bit... well...." Mum sighed and I could tell she was trying to find the right words. It's funny, that. She reads so many books, you'd think she'd have all the words in the world.

I was taking the boys to Denny's rehearsal. Mum didn't want Denny travelling on his own so I had packed Arthur's robot colouring book and my ICT homework. We were late already.

Mum went on. "Only I've been a bit worried. Something's up with you and Sash, isn't it? You can tell me, you know..." Mum had to say it loud over the chug-chugging sound of the bus's engine. I nodded and smiled and turned my face away quickly. I didn't want any fuss, especially not here. I could see Denny disappearing towards The Round Chapel where his rehearsal had started five minutes ago.

Arthur pulled on my arm. "Come *on*, Seren!"

The old dears, Mrs Gold included, smiled, but some of the younger passengers had scowls: the boys with plastic shinpads and football boots on the way to the astroturf, the woman with the shopping trolley, the man with the newspaper and the tattoos. Their scowls were getting bigger by the second. They would be late for the rest of their lives cos my mum had decided now was a good time for a chat.

"I better go," I said. "S'fine. Honest." I smiled again, bigger, sunnier. I didn't want to worry her. "I'll get the tea on. Fishcakes, everyone likes them." I let Arthur pull me off the bus.

"Love you! Love you all!" Mum shouted back at me as the doors folded closed, and I felt myself going red as everyone stared.

I held Arthur's hand tight, and as I walked away down the road I wondered how much Mum had noticed. Even with the latest and most grippingly page-turning Jenny Darling, she would have to be mad not to have realised that Sasha was hardly ever around at home, and how it was between me and her when she was.

You could hear the singing from outside the Chapel. It was round, of course, and old brick, and there were what looked like even older trees planted in front of the building, big and dark and waving their brand-new spring leaves in the wind. Denny had run ahead and I saw him turn and wave at me before he went in.

By the time me and Arthur caught up we could see into the hall. The choir were doing warm-ups, hundreds of Year Sixes going ooo-oooh and aa-ahhh all together. It made me smile. Me and Arthur scurried up the little steps to the gallery that ran round the top of the big hall. There were a few parents and younger kids. Some were running around in between the seats, their mums shushing them uselessly. Down in the hall the Olympic Junior Choir stopped their warm-ups and went quiet.

"We're going to start off with a song you all know."

A man with a straggly beard and funny shoes was standing on a box in front of the kids. "It's *Love is Like a Magic Penny*...." The Year Sixes groaned. It was the cheesiest song ever. A really stupid, cutesy, corny, happy song.

I remembered singing all the time at primary school. Me and Christina both down at the front. We loved singing. Harvest Festival, Diwali, Christmas.

The music teacher would tell us to smile while we sang, so we looked like number one idiots, and I'd be looking back at the parents watching. Sometimes you'd see them crying. Not falling-over sobbing, nothing like that, just the odd tear escaping, or their eyes shining.

I was doing it now, the adult thing I mean. I was standing there, listening, and it felt as if so much of my life was over. I felt as if everything had gone, all that happiness so long ago. I felt like I'd lost so much. Christina, of course, but Sasha, too.

I wiped my eye with the corner of my sleeve.

The song finished and I looked round for Arthur. My insides flipped. He had vanished. There his school bag and his robot colouring book, but no Arthur. I strode around the gallery, looking under the benches and now I wasn't crying, I was angry.

I couldn't shout because they'd hear me downstairs. "Arthur! Arthur!" I hissed.

"Are you all right, love?" one of the mums said.

"Um, no, I've lost my little brother. This tall, brown curly hair."

The woman shook her head. Downstairs the choir had started up *London World in a City*.

I imagined going home and telling Mum I'd lost Arthur. I imagined a whole future in which Arthur was lost and it was all my fault. I imagined never again being able to hear anything to do with the Olympics without thinking of my long-lost little brother. I thought I'd start getting tearful all over again. I took a deep breath and told myself not to be so stupid.

"Arthur!" I hissed again. I went to the steps and ran down to the front door. Outside it was sunny and the new leaves blew about in the trees. The main road was thick with traffic. What if he'd been knocked down by a car? Stuck under a bus like something out of *Casualty*?

"Arthur!" I yelled at the top of my voice. "Arthur!"

He wouldn't be that stupid, would he? If he had been knocked over I reckoned there'd be blue lights, a helicopter ambulance coming in to land on the playground, a crowd standing around at least. There was nothing like that.

I went back into the Round Chapel and up the stairs. Still no sign of him. I took deep breaths and tried to calm myself down. One last look before I called the cops. I scanned the gallery one more time. Nothing. I took out my phone.

Down in the chapel Denny was singing away, unaware that his only brother was gone. I started dialling.

Luckily, I saw Arthur just before I pressed the last nine. There he was, down with the choir, singing his heart out.

"Arthur!" I said, and the whole choir stopped and looked up at me. Straggly-beard man looked daggers. I said sorry over and over again.

I ran downstairs and dragged Arthur back up to the gallery. "What did you go and do that for?"

"It's not fair!" Arthur said. "Why can't I sing too?"

"Your time will come, Art, believe!"

"Want to sing now!" He was really whining. "Why can't *I* sing at the Olympics?"

"I don't know what's up with you, Art, you're never this naughty!"

"I am not naughty!" He stared at me defiantly.

"And you're not my mum!" For a second I thought he was going to do that half-sister thing that Denny had done. But he didn't. It was hard to get him interested in anything in his robot activity book after that.

The bus home was a nightmare. Mum wasn't driving and the boys fought. Other passengers looked at me like I was some deliquent school-girl mother rather than a harassed older sister.

"Denny, your singing is cack-o-rama," Arthur said.

"Don't say that!" Denny snapped back.

"Cackorama, cackorama, cackorama, cackorama, cackorama... did you know cack is spanish for sh–"

"Arthur!" I hissed. "No swearing!"

"I know something!" Arthur said to me in the loudest stage-whisper ever. "I know who Denny likes." Arthur was smiling, his curls framing his face like a naughty cherub.

"Oh yes?" I said. My little brother had a crush? I thought I ought to know.

"Shut up!" Denny's voice was threatening.

Arthur squirmed and giggled.

"Ally- Ally- i-cia…" he sang.

"Shut up!" Denny was suddenly bright red in the face.

"Denny loves Alicia Welsh!" Arthur shouted, and Denny leant across and gave him a chinese burn before I could stop him. Arthur started wailing.

"Denny!" I said, too late.

"You're a baby, Art, you know that," Denny said smugly.

"Am not!" Arthur said, totally baby-like.

"I had my picture in the Gazette and I'll be on the telly all over the world!"

Arthur looked crushed. His little face said 'loser' louder than any words.

"Art, Arthur!" I said. "What about this?" I took the newspaper out of my pocket. "If you entered this, I bet you'd win." I had my fingers crossed.

Arthur looked mildly interested. "Do you win a trip to Disneyland?" he said.

I didn't know. "You get your picture in the paper."

Denny looked across and snorted. "Kutest Kiddie? Arthur would never win."

"Would so!"

"Would not!"

"Would so!"

"WOULD NOT!"

"Boys! Please!" I stared at them with my Vulcan

Death glare. Denny looked at me and curled his lip, and I realised he was totally immune to my scariest face. Outside, the bus had reached the edge of the estate.

"If either of you play up again," I said, in a tone that I hoped was low and deadly, "we are getting off here and walking!"

A whole load of boys got on at the next stop. I felt my insides turn over. One of them was ten-foot-tall Jamie Kendrick. I didn't know any of the others' names but I recognised them all from school, from Sasha's year. The way my afternoon, no, the way my entire life was going, I would put money on Luke Beckford being with them and this journey turning into a massive 'humiliate Seren' fest. I crossed my fingers. I crossed my fingers on both hands and willed them to stay standing near the door, and be so completely wound up in talking to each other that they wouldn't notice me.

What if they did? I took a deep breath. What was the worst that could happen? People laughing at me, saying horrible things? Couldn't I take it? I'd taken it all day. I felt my skin prickle with heat just at the thought. What if they said something to Denny? Or Arthur?

There were only two more stops now.

I opened Arthur's robot colouring book. "Look at that one!" I said.

Arthur gave me his *you are a slug-brain idiot* look.

I could feel Jamie Kendrick trying to make his way through the shoppers to the back of the bus where I was sitting with the boys. I knew it without looking up, from the *excuse mes* and the *sorrys* and the *watch where you're putting your size 12s!*

I stuffed Arthur's book back in my bag. "We are getting off now!" It came out like a snarl and I must have sounded so fierce even Denny didn't argue.

I pressed the bell and we slid out of the door and down into the street.

Arthur looked back at the bus as it sped off. "Seren?" he said.

"Hmm?" I was already walking towards home.

"I think that boy, the giant one, is waving at you."

I didn't look round.

★★★

The house was empty. Mum wouldn't be back for an hour and who knew where Sasha was.

I made the fishcakes. Well, I took them out of the packet and cooked them. I forced Denny to cut up carrots without using the knife on Arthur, and I made Arthur wash some lettuce, otherwise the boys (and me) would never get close to their five a day.

I realised I was starting to think more Mumlike than my actual mum and after tea I went upstairs and turned on the laptop, hoping that the internet would wash over me and make me think like a thirteen-year-old girl with mates again.

I wasn't a friend of Christina's online any more but if I logged in as Sasha I could see her page. I knew it wasn't healthy, I knew it would just make me more miserable, but I had this big need to roll around in my bad feelings and feel even sorrier for myself than I did already.

I hadn't meant to look at Sasha's page. And Keith was sending me a billion messages that made the computer ping like a hyperactive microwave. But I saw it straight away. A picture of me in a heap on the floor of the costume cupboard.

I suppose I ought to thank my lucky stars or maybe my lucky Turkish magic eye that it wasn't a movie, that you couldn't see me shaking or hear the snuffling noises it looked like I was making. I looked totally fishfaced, open-mouthed, red, baggy eyes, ridiculous in a mixture of school uniform and silver sparkles.

Like a broken, spangly puppet.

I felt my heart speed up so fast I thought it would burst. I clicked the page shut immediately.

The messages were pinging into my inbox so noisily they could have been music.

I decided to call Keith.

The first thing he said was, "So you saw it?"

"Did you?"

"It's on Christina's page."

"Oh no! Hers as well? How come you're her friend?"

"She likes to keep her numbers up, I guess."

I clicked the page up again.

"You're looking at it now, aren't you?" Keith said. "Don't be daft!"

"I can't help it. I look so gross."

"Forget it, Seren."

"Forget it?" I was almost yelling. "It's everywhere!"

"You need to think about something else." I heard Keith sigh. "This call will cost you way too much. Message me, no, better still, is Sasha there?"

"She's never here."

"I'm coming round."

I kept Sasha's page up and clicked through to Christina's. Underneath was a long trail of comments from her and Shaz and Ruby and loads of people I had never even heard of. The comments grew as I watched. Christina had commented first:

This is a scene from Keith's crap film where Seren breaks down as she realises she has no friends and no talent.

Then Shazna: **lol. That girl cannot act. Keith is ttl weirdo!**

Then they got harsher. **Seren C-A is a fugly freak** was one of the nicer ones. I took the magic eye out of my drawer and put it around my neck. I was still reading the comments when Keith appeared.

"Right, turn that off. Now," he said, and I did.

"Watch this, and feel better." He clicked over the keys and bought up some of what he'd filmed outside the Olympic park after school. It looked like some science-fiction world of tomorrow and not what had been a building site until what seemed like the day before yesterday.

"Seren? Hello? Lights on and no one's home." Keith waved his hand in front of my face..

"I can't think about anything, Keith," I said. "It's all horrible."

"It's just a picture, Seren. It's just you crying. It's not half as bad as the one of Ed that went up last year.

It could have been much worse."

"Everything could always be worse, Keith. Anyway, it's not the picture so much. It's the comments. They say I'm crap, and you're weird."

"Who'd've guessed? I thought everyone knew that already," Keith said.

I rolled my eyes.

"I didn't read them and neither should you. It's bonkers. It's like torture, you might as well eat broken glass."

"I can't help it. It's like scratching an itch."

"Well, don't!" Keith said.

"I thought all this had finished after last Christmas," I said.

"Christina's obviously got nothing better to do," Keith said. "Come on, Seren, you know what she's like by now. If you'd have been more... I don't know, you do make it easy for her, though."

"How? How do I do that? No, wait, don't tell me," I said, turning the lucky eye over and over in my hand. "I made a fool of myself and I ruined the talent show." I said it quietly.

"Everyone could see she was out to get you! And you didn't ruin the show, just their dance." Keith looked at me. "Christina had engineered it so you'd look crap whatever happened. If you hadn't fallen over she'd probably have pushed you."

I shut my eyes as I remembered going head over heels in front of the whole lower school. The dress I was wearing, a horrible nylon thing nowhere near as nice as Shazna's or Christina's, flipped up and my days-of-the-week-pants were visible to everyone. Everyone.

"No, you're wrong," I said. "You weren't at the rehearsals. She wanted to win."

Keith facepalmed. "She wanted to win without you in the group. You were a bit like some lost puppy, following them around, waiting to be kicked. You wouldn't listen, Seren, you know it." He took a deep breath. "You know that was a low point for me, the rehearsals. I thought you'd stop talking to me then, stop being my mate."

"Why?" I said.

"Because that's what she wanted. You know me by now, Seren, I'm not exactly Mr Sociable. I don't play football, I am entirely uncool, I'm smaller than some of the Year Sevens and my voice probably won't break until I'm forty-five."

I looked at him. I did know all this. I couldn't be Keith's friend and not know all this already. I also knew that I had been a real coward. Christina had wanted me to choose between staying friends with her or Keith, and when I should have told her how vile that was I just tried to be friends with everyone. It wasn't until the talent show that things all came to a head.

Keith was right. I wouldn't take the ten ton 'push-off-and-leave-us-alone-now' hints Christina and Shazna kept dropping. Even Sasha had told me to leave it. She'd tried really hard, she said it was blatant that Christina had had enough of me. We'd been mates so long I couldn't see that it was only because of Sasha and Fay. That Christina had left me behind sometime in the summer holidays after Year Seven, when she did Summer Uni with Shazna while I was helping Dad and Sherifa with the girls.

"They didn't want you any more, Seren, and you wouldn't listen," Keith said.

"I know that!" I said. "Maybe I shouldn't do this film with you, Keith, I'll just ruin it! I can't act!"

"Seren, stop it! Now you are being ridiculous. Christina's just jealous cos you're in my film. She'll get bored. Tomorrow there'll be a photo of a dress she's seen in some shop, or a boy she fancies in Year

Nine, or a kitten making a stupid face!"

I smiled. "So you're on her page rather a lot, then?"

"Totally. It's my favourite site. And you know I would never have asked you to be in the film if I didn't think you were brilliant." He was on the edge of angry and I felt a bit scared looking at him.

"So you'd have asked her or Shazna if you thought she'd be better for your film?"

"Absolutely. But I didn't, did I?"

"No."

"So, no more moaning and no more worrying about what those air-heads think."

"Sorry."

"You shouldn't be sorry."

"Yeah, but everything is going wrong. Everything. And some of that has got to be my fault."

"Look, Seren." He counted off on the fingers of his hand as he spoke. "Those girls are being bitches. You lost a good friend. You tried to help your sister and it went wrong." He shrugged. "That's plenty of stuff."

"I can't stand it, the way it is with me and Sasha. I mean, even Mum has noticed." I wanted to say there was more, loads more, but how much moaning can one person take? There was Dad closing down and moving to Cyprus, and me promising Arthur he'd be the Kutest Kiddie in Hackney...

Keith pushed his glasses up his nose. "I bet you never said anything. To your mum."

"She's got enough on. Work, you know..."

"Yeah, right, and the latest brick of a book she's reading!"

"My mum works hard!" I was angry. It was OK me being cross with Mum, but hearing it from someone else...

Keith put his hands up. "Sorry. I'm just saying. You should talk to her."

I made a huffy noise, but I knew he was right.

"And don't forget you're starring in my totally epic production of *The Tempest* and if you muck that up you'll lose the only friend you've got..."

"Keith, don't joke about it!"

"You won't muck up. And haven't I always been your friend? Even when you and Christina wouldn't let me in your tent?"

"We were eight."

"I have a long memory."

"It was a girls' tent."

"Christina told me I would turn into a girl if I went in. She never liked me, even then."

"I know. I'm sorry. She was horrible to you sometimes."

"Meh." Keith shrugged. "You were never that bad."

"If you were her you wouldn't speak to me now. You wouldn't let me be in your film, even."

"Well, I'm not. And anyway, you're the best at acting in our whole year," Keith said. There was a pause. "Would you let me in your tent now?"

"If I had one."

"That's OK, then."

We were both smiling now.

"Thank you, Keith. Show me your film again."

I thought that if this was a story I would end up falling in love with Keith and riding off into the sunset. But it was never like that with me and Keith, we were just like brother and sister. There were photos of us in the same paddling pool for starters. For seconds I was a good six inches taller than him.

Keith pressed the start arrow. On the screen the sunlight on the water sparkled, and the light seemed alive. The picture on the laptop was more like a moving painting than a film.

"I like this bit," Keith said.

I nodded. "It's beautiful."

"So, you're up for filming tomorrow? At your dad's?"

I nodded again. Then I made a face. "But I don't know about the dress."

Keith rolled his yes. "It looks really good. I shot some of you earlier. Look." He fiddled about with the computer. "There."

It was me posing in the costume cupboard. Because the light was low you couldn't see much of me, but you could see the dress, the sparkles picking up and throwing back points of light, a bit like the water in the canal film.

"See?" Keith said.

"You're right."

"I am always right. Directors are always right. Hitchcock was never wrong."

"Hitchcock?" I said.

"I thought you liked *Strangers on a Train*?"

"I did!"

"He was the director. Did *Psycho* too – the woman in the shower?" Keith made stabby movements with his hand and made that scary music sound. "*Psycho*?"

"I don't read the credits," I said.

Keith pretended to look shocked. "I wonder if there is any hope for you, Seren."

I kissed my teeth.

"I better go." Keith got up. "Tell you what," he said, pointing at the blue glass eye round my neck. "Wear the necklace, it'll keep away the evil eye. It'll look really good close up. Like something magic."

After Keith had gone, Mum came home. I warmed up her fishcake and arranged Denny's carrot sticks. Maybe I could talk to her while she ate. That's what people were supposed to do, talk at the table, not in buses.

"Put the kettle on, love," Mum said, and sat down at our tiny kitchen table in her bus-driver waistcoat. She looked knackered.

I flicked on the kettle and brought her a cup of tea. When I took it over to the table she had out the Jenny Darling and was forking up fishcake.

"You always said reading at the table was bad manners."

"Hmmm?"

"Reading," I said. "At the table."

She shut the book. "Sorry. I was at a really good bit. Did the rehearsal go OK?"

I looked at her. Her eyes were tired and her hair could have done with a brush and a really good condition. My mum's not exactly un-pretty, but the bus-driver outfit never did anyone any favours.

I took a deep breath. I wanted to say, 'No, it didn't go well because I nearly lost Arthur, and they're fighting all the time, and me and Sasha, well, there is no me and Sasha. And who knows what's happening with her exams. I mean, is she revising or what? Does no one care except me? And then my dad is moving away. This family,' I wanted to say, 'is falling apart.' I opened my mouth and her phone went off. She took it out of her pocket.

"Sasha, love!" Mum said. "You're not home?"

From the front room I could hear Denny and Arthur squabbling over the Playstation. I went upstairs. I was down about a minute later. I heard Arthur shouting "Se-ren!" instead of "Mum!", and when I looked, she was sitting in the kitchen lost in Jenny Darling.

★★★

When it was bedtime I read *Room on the Broom* to Arthur for about the millionth time.

"Seren," he said when I'd finished. "I'm sorry."

"What about?" I said.

"This afternoon. I shouldn't have run away and I was loud on the bus. Mum says I should say sorry." He hugged me. He'd managed to talk to Mum, I thought, why hadn't I?

"S'all right." I hugged him back and it felt good. "Good night, Art. Sleep tight. Tomorrow, yeah, you and Den, be nice to each other."

"It's hard, Seren."

"Why?"

"Cos Denny says nasty things. He says we not brothers, he says I came in a box and someone left me on the doorstep."

I smiled. "Sasha used to say that to me too, about the box on the doorstep. He doesn't mean it."

"Did she?" Arthur thought a minute. "Were you?"

"'Course not," I said. "Don't listen to him, he's just winding you up. This is our family, I mean, you and Den, you've even got the same dad." I bit my lip. "Not that it makes a blind bit of difference."

"You're still my sister though, isn't it?"

"You bet." I kissed him on the top of his head. "Totally."

"And Sasha?"

"Yes, too." I kissed him again.

"Then why isn't she here any more?"

"Bedtime," I said. I got up and turned the light off. Even Arthur felt it, even Arthur knew something was wrong.

"Seren?"

"Good night, Arthur."

"Seren, I don't want to be a Kute Kiddie. Denny says it's for babies and I'm not a baby, isn't it?"

I went back to his bunk and sat on the bed again. "No, Art, you're not a baby." I felt for his hand and gave it a squeeze.

"Are you sure?"

"Yes." I ruffled his hair. "I think you'd win," I said.

"But if I didn't it would only be worse," Arthur said. "Denny would tease me more and he would say it was because I was a troll. I want to sing in the Olympics and Denny says the Olympics aren't coming back to London for one hundred and fifty years and then I'll be dead or a head in a bottle that talks like in Futurama, and they still won't want me to sing...."

I tried not to smile. "You can't sing in the Olympics, but you can sing along in the crowd."

Arthur made a huffy noise.

"And you don't have to do Kutest Kiddie if you don't want to..."

"I don't want to. Denny says Cameron and Tyler in my class would beat me up."

"That's awful! You can't let other people stop you doing something if you want to do it! And you are so cute!" I hugged him tight but he pushed me away.

"I don't want to be cute. I want to be Arthur, King of the Britons, like Mum says."

"OK, you don't have to enter the Kute Kiddie thing. But you shouldn't let what other people think stop you doing anything," I said. I sounded a bit like one of those American teens who were always right about everything and went around hugging all the time. Maybe I could still do something....

Perhaps I could send a picture of Arthur in secretly.

I stood in the doorway and watched Arthur get comfy under his duvet. A little flutter of excitement bubbled up inside. I'd send in his picture and then he'd win and be so-o grateful, Mum would be thrilled and even Denny would be proud and maybe Sasha would say something nice to me and want to be my sister again.

I sighed. No, it wasn't worth it. I remembered the last time I tried to do something good. That had rebounded big-time. What if I sent the picture off and then Arthur hated me forever too? How many brothers or sisters could I afford to lose?

Across the landing I could see the light from the

computer screen in my bedroom. I pushed open the door and there was Denny lying on my bed. I was ready to have a go at him. "This is my room!"

Denny was cool. "If I was you, I wouldn't leave the laptop on with you logged in as Sasha." He wagged his finger at me. "Naughty, naughty."

My heart sped up. "Is she here?"

"No, but she could've been." He smiled.

"Give me that!"

Denny moved away from the laptop but he stayed sitting on my bed. What had he seen?

"If you tell her I will kill you!" What if Sasha found out? I scrolled through the history. He'd been looking at game sites. Had he seen my picture? Had he read those comments?

"So what you gonna give me to keep quiet, then? Or I could just spill that I know that you know her passwords..."

"Denny!"

"S'got to be worth something!"

"You know, I was going to have a word with you about Arthur, about how he's so jealous of you, about how he looks up to you so much and you just throw it in his face. He wants to do what you do! He thinks the sun shines out of your..."

"Yeah, well on a good day it does, doesn't it!"

"Denny! I'm trying to talk to you here! Don't forget I'm still three years older than you, Den."

"So? Doesn't mean you should be using Sasha's passwords. Doesn't mean I shouldn't be telling Sasha what you're doing..."

I folded my arms. I remembered the way Denny had gone pink when Arthur mentioned Alicia Welsh.

"OK, Denny, here's the deal. You don't tell Sasha about the passwords. I don't tell Alicia Welsh how much you like her."

The word Alicia did the trick. Denny blanched and now I was smiling.

I was still smiling when he slunk away out of my bedroom, promising his lips were zipped.

I took a deep breath and clicked back to Christina's page. Knowing Denny, he'd have left a really stupid message or something. I scrolled down. There was a picture of a kitten pulling a funny face. I scrolled down some more. The picture of me had gone. I couldn't believe it. I scrolled up and down again. Turned the computer on and off, even unplugged it and booted it up again.

It wasn't there. I skipped across to Sasha's. It had gone from her page too. I checked again. What had happened? Keith and his magic computer skills? No, he wasn't that good. Maybe Christina had had a change of heart? Some people were asking where the picture had gone, but she didn't seem to be replying.

It really had gone. Completely and totally gone. I pictured Christina in her room feeling bad about the nasty comments. After all, she hadn't said any of the really nasty things, had she? Maybe she'd had a word with Fay, who'd said something to Sasha, maybe that's how it was. I wanted to text her, email her to say thank you over and over and maybe forget about Christmas, and even if she didn't want to be best mates like old times, maybe she'd stopped hating me.

The eye was still round my neck. Perhaps it was doing a really good job of keeping away the evil eye. Perhaps it was magic. I would definitely wear it to school tomorrow, under my shirt so none of the teachers noticed, of course.

I still had Christina's number in my phone. I wrote three words, THANK U S, then I retyped SEREN in case she thought it was Shazna, and pressed send.

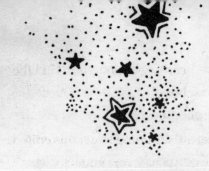

8

IN THE STONE CAVE

I told the story to Keith about ten times on the way to school.

"I think it's this." I waved the eye at him.

"Whatever you say," Keith said. "But just be cool with Christina."

"I don't think I have a cool setting," I said.

"Find it!" Keith pushed his glasses up. "Pretend! Look, if you can pretend to be Miranda, shut away and discovering a brave new world, you can pretend to be someone who is cool."

I thought about it for a bit. We'd reached the big crossing in front of the gate. "You know, Keith, I think you're right again."

"Allow it," he said. "We've got a big day, we've got loads to shoot. We need to do all the café scenes tonight, and then Friday we can get on and do the tower block to keep on schedule."

"You've got a schedule?" I said.

"Of course. How else are we going to get this edited and submitted on time? Whatever you do, don't get detention."

"Yes, boss!" I saluted. "If Miss Tunks says anything to me in Drama I'll keep my mouth shut. I promise. And I'll be so cool, if Christina talks to me she'll think my middle name is Arctic Roll."

But Christina wasn't even in school. I saw Sasha come in with Fay, and for a second she looked at me and I looked straight back and smiled. I felt my heart speed up, and I had to stop myself from calling out or waving, or running over and hugging her. But she looked away after a sliver of a second. I felt incredibly sad: what if Sasha would never want to be my sister again? I imagined a future where Sasha moved out and I had to remind Arthur what she looked like.

So when Shazna and Ruby stared I didn't feel anything at all, which looked as good as cool to the outside world, and me and Keith concentrated on what shots he wanted to get in the café.

115

The café scene came about half-way through the film, when Miranda had made her way down from the tower block and was discovering the world. It was, Keith said, a kind of half-way house – the gateway between the estate and everything else.

"Like a tunnel?" I said, when we were talking it through at lunchtime.

"Exactly!"

"And I have to wear the dress?" I said.

"Of course! The whole point is how the dress reacts to light – just like the water in the canal. It's like a theme: water, change, that kind of thing. The Olympics is a whole new world that she can see and maybe be a part of...." Keith was getting excited.

I didn't say anything because I wasn't sure what he meant. But I did trust him. And I had the dress in my school bag. It was lovely – silver-grey and shiny – like liquid metal, like that stuff they have in thermometers. Mr Demetriou told us all about it once in science. Mercury, he said it was. In the olden days, Mr Demetriou said, they called mercury quicksilver and they thought it was magical.

"It's going to look magic," I said.

"Totally!"

★★★

School crawled by, but at least I stayed off Miss Tunks' radar all the way through Drama. And I didn't say a word even when I got put in a group with Sanjay and Ruby and we had to improvise negative emotions all afternoon. In fact, Ruby was almost a laugh without Shazna telling her what to think. Even Miss Tunks admitted that our group sulk was so the best in the class.

We got the bus to Dad's place and Mum was driving. I wasn't sure if this was a relief or not. Keith still thought I should talk to her, but he didn't realise there was so much she didn't know, so much I hadn't been saying, I wouldn't know where to start. And even if I did tell her, what could she do except worry? It was easier just keeping stuff to myself.

The Stone Cave looked quiet from the high street, and inside it was still empty.

"Seren! Babes!" Dad was at the back of the café, sitting at his laptop. His eyes were all screwed up. "I've left my reading glasses at home," he said. "And is this Keith? Hi, Keith." Dad was smiling.

"Hello, Mr Ali," Keith said.

"Call me Mo."

"Thanks for letting us use your place, Mr Al.., um, Mo."

"Any time, you know you're always welcome," Dad said. "I wish you'd come round more often, bring your mates...."

Keith looked at me and we both said, "Nene," out loud, at the same time, and laughed.

"Is she that bad?" Dad said, and I nodded. He made a face.

Dad made Turkish coffee for us all, which Keith couldn't drink, and even though I hadn't spelt it out to Dad about the filming he was in such a good mood we could have danced around on the tables and he and Mehmet would have moved them into place to make it easier.

It went really well. Keith filmed me looking as if my brain had dribbled out of my ears (that is, mouth half open), as I walked from the back of the cave to the big glass door, running my hand across the fake stone and glittering in the low lighting in my silver frock. He did close-ups of hands, close-ups of eyes, close-ups of the fringy bits on the frock as it fringed while I walked, and close-ups of the big, blue glass eye.

Keith was well pleased with the rushes and we sat at the back eating a free sandwich, watching them in the tiny flipped-out screen. Dad leaned over and watched too, although without his reading glasses I wondered how much he could actually see.

"Keith, that looks really good!"

"Thanks, Mr Ali. I'll make sure the Stone Cave gets on the credits."

"See that, Mehmet?" He called Mehmet over, and made him watch the footage too. "My daughter has such talented friends!"

I smiled.

"Seren is talented too," Keith said.

"Oh, I know that!" Dad gave me a hug.

"Shame Nene doesn't," I said.

"We love you, Babes, me and Sherifa and the girls. That's what matters." He grinned at Keith, who was going as red as the ketchup sachets on the table.

"So you promise you won't all go and vanish off to Cyprus, then?"

Dad said nothing. He could have just denied it, out right. 'Of course not,' he could have said, but he didn't. He looked away. He might as well have waved the tickets in my face.

Half of me wanted to ask him when this was happening exactly, and the other half wanted to pretend I never knew. The conversation dried up, and even the police siren going up the main road wasn't loud enough to fill up the silence. Cyprus. Nene had got what she wanted, and I would lose my dad.

"So!" Keith said brightly. "Did you get in touch with Violet, at the Rio, Mr... Mo?"

Dad looked blank.

"She's the manager at the Rio, the cinema. Seren said you might need her number."

"Oh, yes, the cinema," Dad said. "Yeah, well, I've been dead busy."

I looked round the empty cafe. "Yeah, right."

"She's really nice, Violet is," Keith said.

"Dad! You should call her. She might be able to put some business your way," I said. "It's got to be worth a try." I folded my arms. "Unless, of course, you don't care and you want to just sell the café and go to Cyprus!"

"Seren, I have sweated blood for this place!"

"But Nene...."

"But nothing!" He shifted in his seat. "Anyway, the Rio is full of students, isn't it? Hmm? Those arty types with dirty shoes and messy hair and bits of metal in their faces."

"Dad! I have been going to the cinema club since I could walk!"

"And me," said Keith, who still had his school tie on and looked about as unmessy as you can get, even after a whole day at school.

Dad went on. "And do you, or those arty types, have any money to spend on a meal out? No. I rest my case."

I wanted to tell him that 'those arty types' have taken over the café in the park so that now it only sells organic sausages that cost about a tenner each and ice cream made from 100% smiley cows, but I didn't.

Dad turned back to his computer spreadsheets and started tapping. If I could get him to see the Stone Cave could make some money, maybe he'd think twice about packing up.

"Keith?" I said. "D'you reckon Violet's around now?"

Keith nodded. "She practically lives there, anyway." He checked the time on his watch. "The matinees will have all finished and they'll be getting ready for the evening show. Now would be perfect!"

"Dad," I said, and stood up, holding his hand. "Look I promise not to go on about it any more if you just come with us. Now. Please?"

Dad sighed. We looked at each other for what seemed like ages, but I wasn't giving up. Eventually his face softened, he folded the laptop shut, and I smiled.

" Mehmet!" I shouted. "We're taking Dad down the Rio. We'll be five minutes!"

I practically pulled him out of the café and down the road before he could change his mind.

★★★

Keith went ahead. The main doors were shut but he knew where the side bell was, and soon a tall man with an afro was letting us in.

"Keith! How's it runnin'?" he said, and him and Keith touched knuckles like the Obamas and Luke Beckford's mates do. The tall man waved at me. I sort of knew him, he was the projectionist and he let Keith watch him work sometimes.

"Hi, Kes," I said, hoping I'd remembered his name. "This is my dad."

Dad smiled, and for a second I was worried he was going to start Hi-fiving or something embarassing. But he didn't, and Keith asked for Violet, and Kes said she was in the cinema on her rounds, and that we could wait in the cinema.

Keith and Kes went up to his projectionist's booth, and me and Dad went into the empty cinema to look for Violet. The lights were on and we could see her across the rows of seats, a small woman with short, scruffy hair.

"See! They're all hippies!" Dad muttered. But I shushed him up and we walked across.

The Rio wasn't like one of those multi-screen places. It was a proper, old-fashioned cinema with a stage and comfy, red velvet seats and only one screen. One big screen behind red velvet curtains.

"Seren, isn't it?" she said. "Keith's friend?"

"Yeah, I am." I was about to tell her about Dad and the café when the cinema lights started down and the curtains hummed and creaked open. The rectangle of screen lit up in a flash of white light, and I could hear Keith shouting from the projectionist's booth, "Check this out!"

Suddenly, in the square of light on the massive cinema screen, our film, Keith's film, the one he shot just minutes ago in the café was running, huge and glowy. I was about ten foot tall and my hair was black as the dark all around us, and the silver dress shone and glittered like water under moonlight. Nothing much happened. I wandered through the café about ten times looking dim, and there was no sign of a story, not yet, but it did look amazing.

I felt Dad's arm round my shoulders and he squeezed me close. "You look great, Babes," he whispered.

Just as suddenly the film stopped. Violet clapped and I heard whistling, probably Kes, from the projection booth.

"Wow!" said Violet. "Is that Keith's entry?"

"It's just the rushes!" Keith yelled.

"Yeah, he shot that stuff just now, so it's nowhere near finished," I said.

Violet turned to my dad. "That boy has so much potential! And Seren, you looked fantastic!"

"S'not really proper acting," I said. "Not yet."

Suddenly my dad jumped sideways, "Oh my God!" A streak of tabby fur shot out from beneath his feet. "What was that?" he said. My dad is not an animal fan. He thinks pets are a daft English invention and all animals should live outside.

"Oh, that's just Derek," I said. "The cinema cat."

"He works here too," Violet said, and I could see Dad thinking 'hippies' again.

"Derek?" Dad said. "That's not a cat's name."

"Yeah, he's named after a film director," said Violet. "Good mouser though."

"Violet," I said. I had to bring the conversation back

to business. "My dad runs the Stone Cave."

"The Stone Cave! I love that place!" she said and Dad smiled. They started talking about the Turkish Film Festival and films I had never heard of.

"The Mothers and Babies?" I said, trying to get them back on track. "I had this idea."

Violet looked at me.

"Dad was thinking about doing coffee and cake and that."

Dad looked mildly embarassed.

"I mean," I said, "I know you do teas and coffees and that in the foyer, but there's nowhere for the mums to chat really, and it would make sense cos Dad's got the space and maybe he could run a creche or something, so the mums could hold their hot cups away from the babies and that...." I was gabbling again. I should really know when to shut up.

"You know what?" Violet said. "That's not an entirely bad idea."

Before we left, Dad and Violet had made a date for another meeting and things were looking quite rosy. Keith was staying to help Kes with the evening feature, so I walked back to the café with Dad.

"You are quite something, you know that?" Dad said.

"I like to think so."

"Maybe I should make you my agent. You're not a bad businesswoman. I mean, I know it's not signed and sealed, but maybe we're looking at a few more punters, and that's all we need." Dad raked his hand through his hair. "Look, don't say anything to your sister, cos we're a long way from being able to give her her job back, but this might just be the leg-up the Stone Cave needs."

"So long as you stay here, and don't move away. That's all I care about, Dad."

"The way things are going, you'll probably be raking in the dollars in Hollywood and taking care of your old dad before you know it."

"I don't think so!"

"Look, why don't you come round to the house tomorrow, after achool, the girls would love to see you. Sherifa hasn't seen you for months!"

"Nene...." I said.

"She'll be here, at work with me. Sherifa can take you three out somewhere, if you want. I mean, after today, it's the least I can do."

"I'll check with Mum, but if it's OK, tell Sherifa I'll be over for half six."

Dad kissed me on the cheek. I walked down to the

bus stop happier than I'd felt for a long time. The film looked brilliant and Dad was cooking up some kind of deal with the Rio. I crossed my fingers. If he could stay open until the Olympics, maybe he wouldn't go at all.

Things were definitely getting better. I told myself this could be the beginning of some good stuff. I imagined going home and Sasha smiling at me. I imagined Christina seeing me ten foot high on the big screen at the Rio. I smiled.

9

HAPPY FAMILY

Dad and Sherifa lived just round the corner from the Stone Cave, in a terraced house, with a little front gate and a rose bush in front of the window. I walked down the road thinking that when I was grown up I wouldn't mind living in a place like this. There were big, old trees that nodded at each other on either side, all the windows of the houses looked across at each other like rows of kids sat down at huge, long dinner tables.

Sherifa wore nice clothes – she worked down Canary Wharf in an office – and the girls always had loads of stuff. You know, the right Barbies and Bratz for birthdays, that kind of thing. They almost seemed like a family out of an advert, fluffy rugs and no food dropped on the floor or anything.

I knocked at the door and looked up at the house.

There weren't any lights on. Was nobody in? I checked the time on my phone. I was only a tiny bit early. I stepped on to the flower bed and looked into the front room through the living-room window. If I stood right next to the glass I could see through the net curtains. Maybe I'd see Ayse and Gamze dancing along to *High School Musical* like mini Gabriellas.

But the room looked different. Empty. There was a huge gap where the TV was, and the massive professional photo of Sherifa and the girls, all dressed in white tops, that hung over the fireplace, wasn't there. The sofa was covered in some kind of dustsheet and there was a step ladder up in the far end of the room. What was going on? They couldn't have packed up and moved to Cyprus already, could they?

I rang the doorbell again. Hard. Nothing happened.

Half six, Dad had said. Maybe he'd even forgotten to say anything to Sherifa at all. Maybe this was some plot of Nene's. I took my phone out and clicked through my contacts. I had just got down to S when their silver people-carrier pulled up in front of the house.

"Seren! I am so sorry!" Sherifa hugged me hello. In the back seats I could see the girls strapped in.

"Ohmigod! I am so sorry, we are running late. I had to pick the girls up from their mates'." She checked her watch. "And we should be at Drama. Now."

I hovered on the doorstep while Sherifa shot in, picked up a bag and shot out again.

"Seren, get in, we'll drop the girls, then I'll take you out."

I climbed into the passenger seat and waved at the girls. I thought they had grown so much, but I didn't say it in case I sounded like some old lady.

"I'll be in Year Six next year!" Gamze said.

"I thought you did Drama on a Wednesday?" I said.

"No." Sherifa drove back up the road to the High Street. "That's Music, or is it Dance?"

"Mum!" said Ayshe. "It's Dance on Wednesday and Music on Saturday."

"Trampolining on Monday!" said Gamze.

"When do you get to veg out in front of the telly?" I said.

"Oh, they still manage to get enough TV time, believe me," Sherifa said.

We didn't drive for long. In fact, I thought we could have walked it quicker, cos the traffic in the High Street was solid. Sherifa pulled into a tiny street I'd never seen and there was a theatre. Honest. A proper theatre. I thought it was just an old warehouse first, but round the entrance were posters – the play they had on was called *The Cherry Orchard*, and one of the actresses in it had been on the telly, cos I recognised her picture.

"I never knew this was here!" I said.

"Yeah, the Arcola. It's brilliant. One of my mates set it up, they just bought this old coat factory and practically built it themselves."

I was speechless. Why didn't I know about it?

"And they do great classes," Sherifa said. "Don't they, girls?"

The girls looked particularly unexcited. Ayshe was combing her Bratz doll's hair and Gamze looked as if she would rather be somewhere, anywhere, else.

"You love it, don't you, girls?" Sherifa said brightly.

They so didn't. I could see that a mile off.

The classes weren't in the main theatre, but in studios upstairs. The girls were both in the middle age group, 7-12s. On the way up we passed an older group. I looked in through the square glass window. About ten kids my age. I would have given anything to go in.

Instead I walked up another flight with Sherifa and watched as she apologised for being late. Ayshe really didn't want to go and I felt sorry for the two tutors.

"Right, Seren, we've got the best part of an hour. I said to your dad I'd take you out. How about a dash round the shops in Spitalfields? Whatever you want. We can come and pick the girls up on the way home."

Sherifa looked tired too. Although she had good make-up on, there were dark circles under her eyes. When Mum looked like that, really done in after a shift on the buses, the last thing she wanted was to go round the shops. What worked for her was the latest Jenny Darling and a cup of tea. And even though the idea of a lush new top was great, I knew I'd really rather just hang out here.

"Tell you what, Sherifa," I said. "Why don't you go home and put your feet up. I'll hang out here and bring the girls home."

Sherifa looked shocked. "On your own? It's dark now."

"Come on, it's not far, and I'd love a look in at the older class."

"Seren, darling, they're not just going to let you

walk in. I mean, we had the girls down on waiting lists for months."

"I know, but you've been at work all day, and I've been at school. Thanks for the offer, for the shopping and that, though."

"You're sure?" Sherifa looked as if she couldn't wait to get back into the car.

I nodded.

★★★

After she'd gone I went back to the older class. They looked as if they were doing some kind of improvisation in four groups. The sort of thing we do in school, but all the kids here were really good. I thought I recognised a boy from my school, from Year Ten, but I wasn't sure. There weren't any Sanjays or Eds mucking around, no Christinas with hands like plastic spoons. They all wanted to be there. I took three deep breaths and pushed the door open, and went in. Everyone stopped and looked.

"Can I help?" One of the tutors smiled at me. I knew he was a tutor because he was older, with a bit of a beard.

I pretended I had loads of confidence and smiled back. The groups went back to their work.

"Seren Campbell Ali," I said. "I was wondering if I

could, you know, watch, or maybe join in? I'm just visiting, I've got sisters in the other class." I said it quickly so he wouldn't stop me and chuck me out.

I saw the tutor flick a look at a woman – the other tutor – but he showed me a seat. I couldn't help feeling a tiny bit disappointed. I would have loved to join in, to be a part of it. But then these kids probably had parents who could afford to pay whatever the classes cost. Mum had never been able to fork out for extras. We'd never had all those singing and dancing and breathing lessons my two little sisters had. We did all the free stuff in the summer holidays. You know, in the libraries or at the swimming pool. I'd even done Drama one time with Summer Uni but it was full of girls who wanted to be Hannah Montana. It was nothing like this.

All the groups came up with brilliant scenes. The performances were so good! So much better than school. They'd been given the theme of 'endings' and every group's performance was different. One group acted as a class of Year Elevens on the last day of school, another was a family breaking up, mother leaving father.

My favourite was the scene the last group did. It was two brothers arguing over who would inherit the family farm. One shouted horrible things at the other, hurting, hateful things, and suddenly I felt my throat dry and catchy, and I thought I was going to cry.

I realised I felt so choked up because it made me think of me and Sasha, and I knew, more than anything, that I had to make it up with Sasha, even if she didn't want me to. Even if I couldn't see how to do it right now.

The time went so fast, I suddenly realised the girls' session was over. I dashed upstairs and took hold of one bored, tired little girl in each hand and dashed back to try and talk to the tutors.

"Just wait, I won't be a second," I said. Ayshe looked as if she could curl up on the hard, plastic chair and fall asleep right there.

"Excuse me again," I said, and asked about the class. If this had been on telly it would have happened like this. He would have let me join in the class, seen how absolutely fantastic I was at acting and asked, no, begged, me to come every week for nothing. But as this was real life he just gave me a leaflet.

We walked back in the dark and the girls really perked up.

"Don't you want to do Drama, then?" I said.

"Classes are boring," Ayshe said. "They go on and on."

"Gabriella in *High School Musical* does Drama, I bet," I said.

"No, Dur-brain! Gabriella does Maths! She does Science! She doesn't do Drama!"

"Ayshe," Gamze said, all big-sister know-it-all. "Gabriella is fictional."

That was me told.

We got back to the house and the girls ran in through the wood-floored hall and away upstairs, each begging me to come and see her bedroom first.

Sherifa was in the kitchen stirring something in a saucepan, drinking a glass of red wine. "You must come more often. When things aren't in such a rush."

"Isn't it like this all the time? The girls said they have classes every night," I said.

"It keeps them busy. And me and your dad have too much work."

"He does seem really tired at the moment, Dad."

Sherifa shot me a look.

"Oh and you do too, you both do. I bet you're both working very hard." I was starting to gabble. I took a breath. "Couldn't Nene have them more often?"

Sherifa looked at me again and made a face, and I smiled. "Oh," I said.

"Oh. Exactly. Would you want your daughters spending more time with her than absolutely necessary?"

"I thought it was just me," I said.

"Oh no!" Sherifa said, "I am the devil in human form as far as Nene is concerned."

"Now you're way off. That is my mother."

We laughed. She told me some of the things Nene had said about her drinking. "I have the odd glass of wine. If you listened to her you'd think I was on my back in the gutter draining crates of the stuff! And of course she hates me working. Very traditional is Nene. Can't stand it that I earn more than your dad." Then Sherifa told me how Nene also hated the way they brought up the girls, and banged on about how they should all move to Cyprus with her.

"Ohmigod!" I suddenly remembered the empty front room. "You're not moving, are you? Only Mehmet in the cafe was sort of talking about it, and Dad's been really funny and given my big sister the sack...."

"Slow down, love. Listen, we are not going anywhere. Especially not to Cyprus with Nene. Wild horses would have to drag me. I don't mind a holiday, in the spring when it's not too hot, but all year round? No way! I know your dad's been a bit... well... I don't know how long he can keep that place open."

"So you're not packing up and moving?"

"Whatever gave you that idea?"

I told her everything, about the front room, about knowing the restaurant was losing money and that Dad might have to sell up. "I thought he'd leave me and I'd never see him again."

Sherifa smiled. "Oh, Seren! Love! That's not it at all. We're just having the front room redecorated." She came over to me and took my hand. "And another thing. Your dad loves you. He wouldn't leave you. I know he's got me and the girls, but you're special to him, you know that. And to me for that matter."

I wanted to say, 'No, I don't know that.' I wanted to say, 'Gamze and Ayshe get classes in stuff they don't want and holidays in the sun and I get nothing.' But I didn't. I did say, in a small, six-year-old's voice, "If you went to Cyprus I'd never see him because Nene would be there all the time."

"Seren, when that woman has gone, my life, our lives, will be much easier, you know that."

Sherifa told me again that no way would they ever

be moving. Nene, however, was moving just as soon as she sold her flat in Wood Green, and she had tried, and failed, to persuade the whole family to go with her.

"Your dad might have to sell, love, but believe me, he's not going anywhere."

"Are you sure?"

"Not if I have anything to do with it. Have you seen the jobs available in northern Cyprus? It would be a miracle if I got something that paid half as well out there." Sherifa hugged me tight. She smelled delicious: perfume, cooking and red wine. I felt exhausted.

I wanted to go home. But I played two rounds of *High School Musical* the computer game with the girls, out of sisterly duty, first.

On the bus on the way back I read the leaflet. Arcola Theatre Youth Drama Group. Seniors, 13-18. How much did it cost? I flipped the leaflet and read, Classes cost £20 for a 12-week term. That worked out at less than £2 a week. I imagined the future, with Nene in Cyprus, and Sherifa paying me to babysit or take the girls to Music or Dancing or Origami or whatever, and me going to Drama classes. Nene was leaving! I leant my head against the glass and shut my eyes and smiled.

10

FREAKY FRIDAY

I hardly saw Sasha, not at school or at home. I had used her computer to send an email to the theatre about classes and they emailed back almost right away. I was on the list for next term!

Keith said he thought it was a brilliant idea about Drama classes. He said I looked much happier, and I told him what had happened with my dad and what Sherifa said.

"See, Seren? Isn't that what I said? You have to talk to people! You should talk to your mum too. I bet she is so worried, just cos you've been worried."

"She doesn't notice a thing," I said.

"Liar," Keith said. "And you have to talk to Sasha."

"I know that!" I said. "You're supposed to be less I-told-you-so and more matey-supporty."

"Yeah, but I was right, wasn't I?"

"Yes, Keith, yes, you were."

"As I said before, I am your Director and I am always right."

"Keith," I said. "You are asking for it, you know that?"

We walked over to the estate where we were going to film the scene where Miranda comes down in the lift.

"I'll see how it looks. You might have to do the stairwell too, if it doesn't work out."

"Thanks for that, Keith," I said.

"It's great for your thighs," Keith said, and got out of the way so I didn't hit him.

★★★

We were filming on the Arden estate. I know people have this idea of Hackney as being full of council estates and tower blocks overrun with gangster hoodies and teenage mothers. Believe it or not, that is so not true. Mum told me how they blew up most of the tower blocks years ago, and the newer estates, like ours, are all red and yellow brick.

But the Arden estate was a sort of throwback. It was what most people think of when they say 'estate'. It had one white tower, and a lot of low-rise blocks on concrete legs that you could walk through or hide behind. It wasn't like a war zone or anything, but I'd probably have thought twice before I walked through it at night.

The tower was fifteen storeys high, and had a nasty metal box of a lift which smelt of disinfectant. After we'd been up and down ten times though, I stopped noticing. I had to go up on my own and Keith waited for me on the floor below, filming me as I stepped out.

Then we went up to the top floor, and looked west across the city and my heart almost stopped, we were so high up. The city was spread out all around for miles and miles. As if it never ended. To the west was a sort of tourist view of London, with a slice of St Paul's and the Gherkin, in between the pointy fingers of the city skyscrapers.

"Amazing!" I said. And I looked round to the north, where what was left of the marshes was criss-crossed with circles of tyre marks from scooters and motorbikes, like the biro lines you make with a Spirograph.

Then we walked round to the other side of the block and we could see all across to the east.

The Olympic Park looked like a giant plastic toy, a city made by Lego or Fisher Price, spread out on a carpet of bright green grass. I could just see the shine on the river Lea as it snaked through the park, like a gold ribbon.

Keith took out his camera and started filming.

I looked down into the courtyard far below. The people were tiny, not much bigger than ants. I saw a woman with a pushchair loaded up with shopping bags, two boys kicking a bright orange dot of a ball and a girl, with a sort of familiar walk, striding across the concrete...

I knew who that was. It was Sasha, it had to be.

I followed her with my eyes and strained to make out her brown hair piled up on top of her head. With every step the girl took I was more sure it was Sasha.

"Shall I go down there?" I said. "You could film me in the courtyard from up here. I could look sort of lost... It might work."

"Great idea," Keith said, not looking away from the flip-down screen.

The lift seemed to take forever and when I did make it down to the bottom the girl who I thought might have been Sasha had vanished. My phone went off but it was just Keith telling me to act disorientated. I

143

had to get him to explain what it meant and eventually he said, "What you just said, kind of lost."

Down on the ground, in between the blocks, the wind was vicious, and I had to shut my eyes to stop the grit and dust that tried to blow into my eyes.

I wandered around looking like a well-meaning nutter, getting laughed at by the football boys, until Keith came down and showed me what he'd done on the little screen.

Then the football boys came over to look too. And suddenly they were all over Keith wanting to be in his film, and asking him how much his camera cost. I started to worry that the football boys might have older, bigger brothers who might be even more interested in the camera.

Keith was obviously thinking the same thing because he got up at the exact same time as me. "We better go," he said. And we walked back towards the bus stop. But he couldn't help flicking the camera on and running through the stuff we'd just shot as we walked. I slowed and watched too. The colours seemed brighter in the dark under the flats. The little picture shone, it was almost magic.

"What about the people who make flames come out of their fingers?" I said. "How are you going to do that?"

"Oh, one of my cousins does classes at Circus Space. He's got a mate who does stuff with fire."

I was about to ask what he meant when he stopped. There was the tinny roar of motorbikes coming fast behind us.

Keith bundled the camera into his bag and whispered, "Don't look round! Just walk on!"

He looked terrified. He moved the rucksack with the camera from his back round to his front, but fumbled and dropped it just as the bike boys sped past. A can of Coke, a bag of white-rabbit sweets and the camera, carefully wrapped in Keith's school jumper, tumbled out on to the street.

I gasped. "Is it all right?"

Keith was getting wound up. He was all fingers and thumbs until he was sure the camera worked.

"I thought they were going to jack us," he said. "It happens, they come up behind you and take your bag. Miss Tunks would have killed me."

"No, she would have killed *me*," I said.

"Hang on," Keith said, stopping. "Isn't that Sasha?"

"Where?"

Keith pointed to a couple standing up against one of the concrete pillars, practically glued together. No mistake, it was Sasha. She was wearing her favourite blue top, and her brown hair was snaking down her back in springy brown curls. She had her head bent up at what looked like a very tricky angle because she was kissing a hugely tall boy.

"Oh my days!" I said.

"Jamie Kendrick!" Keith said out loud. "Looks like she's got herself a date for the Leavers' Prom after all."

I yanked Keith back behind the nearest pillar.

"What are you doing?" he said.

"They might see us!"

"So?"

"She'll think I'm spying on her or something!" I whispered. "She'll think we're stalking them. Ohmigod! Put the camera away! Now! She'll think we're filming!" I practically pulled the camera out of Keith's hands and stuffed it back into the bag.

"Careful!" Keith was losing patience. "Seren! Calm down! Why would I want to film your sister and Jamie Kendrick?"

I could picture her storming over, telling me all sorts, accusing me of ruining her life all over again.

"She hates me, OK? We just have to get out of here. Quickly, without them noticing," I said. I could see the bus stop ahead, and coming round the curve of the road from the junction was a little red bus.

"Seren, I don't think either of them would notice if the sky fell in."

He had a point. Given that Jamie and Sasha were glued together, if me and Keith made like Usain Bolt and got on the bus they wouldn't know we were here. But I wasn't taking any chances.

"The bus! Now!" I pulled Keith along after me and sprinted for the bus stop, one hand on Keith's arm, one arm stuck out in front of me hailing the bus like it was life or death. I was in luck, we made it and the bus doors squeaked open.

I was totally out of breath. Me and Keith swiped our cards and I looked round in case I could see Sasha, but she was in love-land and hadn't noticed a thing. I grinned at Keith and we flopped down on the back seats.

"What was that about?" Keith said.

"I said, I didn't want them to see us," I wheezed.

"I got that. A bit extreme, no? I don't get what else she could do to you?"

I took some more deep breaths. "It's just easier like this." I thought for a minute, then looked at Keith. "Jamie Kendrick!" I said.

"You are mad, you know that?" Keith said.

We were almost home, just passing the marshes.

The trees all had their new leaves and the colour was fresh, bright green, like school powder paint.

Keith must have thought so too. "That would look good," he said, and took the camera out of his bag. He clicked it on.

I saw the colour drain from his face. He went from normal Keith to paper-white in seconds.

"What's up?" I said.

Keith patted his pocket. Then he patted his other pocket. He stood up and patted everywhere.

"What is it?" I said again. I was getting nervous just watching him. "The camera? Is it OK?"

Keith said nothing. He stood up again. He emptied his pockets out and now he took everything out of his rucksack. The camera was there, his notebook, and school jumper.

"What is it, Keith?"

Keith pressed the bell to stop the bus at the next stop and walked down to the door. I followed him.

"Keith, what's happened?"

The bus slowed and the doors opened, and Keith stepped off and began to walk back to the Arden estate. He didn't look back at me, but I followed him. I'd never seen him like this in ten years of friendship. Keith was always cool, always calm. I'd never seen him angry, even back at that time when Christina wouldn't let him in the tent.

"Talk to me, Keith!"

He didn't slow down. His voice was sharp. "The memory stick. It's gone."

"What?"

"You heard me!" Keith had stopped and was facing me. "I've lost the bloody memory stick."

"But you had it outside the flats. It must be in your bag." I tried to keep cool. "We were just watching...."

"Well, it's not there now! You pulled me along, remember?" He pointed at me. "You made me run. It must have come out then. Everything is on it. The whole film. Everything."

I felt sick. For a long second we stared at each other, Keith had never looked at me so viciously. Lots of other people had, plenty of times, but not Keith.

"It's gone," he said. "I'm going back to the bus stop."

"Are you sure?" I said, but Keith had already started jogging along the road back to the Arden estate. I caught up with him. "We'll find it, Keith, I know we will, don't worry."

Keith pushed past me. I ran to catch up. Even though he was smaller than me he was moving very fast.

When we got to the low-rise block he retraced our steps between the tower block and the bus stop, head down, eyes glued to the pavement. I did too. I kept an eye out for Sasha, but her seeing me didn't seem to matter at all now. I saw the football boys and asked them if they'd seen anything, but I got the feeling they wouldn't have told me even if they had.

Keith wasn't speaking at all now, and it was starting to get dark.

"Can't we just do it again?" I said.

It was like the worst thing I could have ever said. Keith exploded. "You idiot! We'll never get the light like that again, never! If you hadn't made me run, if you hadn't been so stupid!"

"Keith," I said. It came out very quiet.

"Like I said, this was your fault."

"Hold on a minute!" I said. "You dropped the bag, remember? It could have happened then!"

"If you hadn't flustered me..."

"No. I was helping, you were flustered."

"You pulled me!" he shouted.

"You dropped the bag!" I shouted back.

We looked at each other. He was half-way between anger and tears. He suddenly looked much younger.

"How could you say it was my fault?" I tried not to be so loud.

Keith just walked away. "Leave me alone!"

I watched his back disappear down towards the canal. After a while I started walking back the way we had come, hoping I'd find his stupid memory stick and then I'd be able to go round to his and tell him the good news. I walked all round the estate again until my feet hurt. I even looked in the gutter.

But the gutter smelt and I was cold in the grey dress and it was getting darker. I would have to go home.

I put my school jumper on over the top and went back to the bus stop. I saw my reflection in the plastic glass of the bus stop and realised I'd rubbed the mascara I'd put on for the shoot, all round my eyes. I looked like a glittery panda. I rubbed at my face some more with the sleeve of my jumper trying to get the worst of it off, but it just made my eyes red.

I had just tried to call Keith for the millionth time when the bus came swinging round the corner.

Keith wasn't answering. It wasn't like him at all.

11

A LONG RIDE HOME

"Oh, Seren, love!" Mum said. She almost sounded hurt herself. "What happened?" She lowered her voice, but everyone on the bus could still hear. "Have you been crying?"

"No! No, I haven't. S'all right, Mum." I wiped at my face some more. I swiped my card and walked to the back of the bus, like normal, but the bus didn't move.

"Seren!" Mum called out to me.

The whole bus was staring now and I felt my face heat up. I walked back to the front of the bus, squeezing past the buggy, almost tripping over a man with an umbrella.

Mrs Gold smiled at me from the priority seats as I passed. "Darling, you go and talk to your mum, there's a good girl," she said.

I bit my tongue. "Mum!" I said. "Really, I'm fine. Drive the bus!" I tried to keep my voice as low as I could.

Mum sighed and the bus began to move off.

"Thank you," I said, and started to move back to my seat.

"No, love, stay put. Please! I can see something's wrong." She said it loud and the whole bus was listening.

I said nothing. If my mum had driven the big buses, the proper double-deckers or the massive bendy ones, I would have been able to get out of earshot.

"You can't hide it, love," Mum called out again as two new passengers got on. "You need to talk to me, Seren."

I made a face. This was mad.

The boys in the seats near the front were giggling. I folded my arms. I wished I had my MP3 player so I could put my earphones in and block everything out.

"I am fine!" I shouted back. I stared out of the window hard, as if the *Perfect Fried Chicken* and the betting shop we were passing were fantastically interesting. I knew the whole bus was looking at me. Mrs Gold, the boys, a woman with shopping, an old man with a stick. I felt them all staring. I felt hotter and redder every second. I should never have got on the bus.

"Seren? Please!"

The boys burst out laughing.

Mum yelled, real anger in her voice. "And you two can shut up!"

The boys just laughed more and louder.

Mum said my name again and I realised she wasn't going to give up, I got out of my seat and stood next to her driver's cab. "Mum, don't shout!" I hissed. "You're embarassing me."

Mum had her eyes on the road, concentrating on the traffic, but she was flicking little sideways looks at me. What if she crashed and that was all my fault too? Although I couldn't help thinking that those boys laughing at me probably deserved to die.

"We need to talk," Mum said. The dashboard was covered with photos of me and Sash and the boys, all grinning away in our various school uniforms. I thought if she was more honest there ought to be a bigger picture of Jenny Darling.

"Look, Mum," I said quietly. "I am fine. Completely, totally fine! If you want to talk, why don't we do this at home? Oh, wait, I forgot, you're either not there or you're buried in a bloody book!"

We were at the traffic lights across from the high

street and the bus's engine was chugging away. She looked at me as if she might burst into tears. She took one hand off the steering wheel and reached across. I moved away.

"Oooo-ooo," went the boys, all together.

The lights turned green and the bus lurched forward.

"Right!" Mum said, and she steered the bus against the kerb and slammed on the brakes. I nearly fell into Mrs Gold's lap. "We're talking now!" She pulled on the handbrake. "Right now."

"Mum!" I said. "What are you doing?"

There was a low, upset mumbling from the passengers.

Mum turned round and spoke to them. "You lot! You lot especially!" She looked at the boys and they laughed, but this time it was nervous laughter. "You can get off my bus!" She came out from her driver's seat and opened the doors, and started shoo-ing the passengers off, like they were sheep. "Go on! Go! Out!"

"You can't do this!" said walking-stick man, waving his stick.

"You're having a laugh! I paid my ticket!" said shopping-bag woman.

The boys swore at her and said she was mad.

Mrs Gold said, "Linda, are you all right?"

"Fine, Eva. It's just I need to talk to my Seren. And I think I've let a couple of things get in the way." She went back to the driver's seat, and while the passengers muttered and moaned she radioed the bus garage and asked for another bus to pick up her passengers.

"Mum, you can't! What if you get the sack? Mum! This is mad!"

But Mum said nothing. She flicked on the bus's hazard lights and the bus was filled with a reflected orange, on-off glow.

The passengers grumped off the bus. The boys swore even more. The woman with the shopping was on about writing a letter of complaint. The man with the stick said this was exactly the reason why women shouldn't be allowed to drive buses as they let their families get in the way of everything. Then the woman with the shopping started a row with him and I wouldn't have been surprised if she ended up knocking his stick away.

Mrs Gold pushed herself up off her seat,

"Eva, you stay put," Mum said, and closed the doors on the empty bus. "I'll run you home after." Mrs Gold smiled and sat back down.

"Don't mind me," she said. "I'm practically deaf."

Mum turned the sign that normally read Homerton Hospital and set it to something else. I couldn't see what but I expect it said, Not in Service.

"Come and sit down, love." She sat down at the back of the bus where the blow heater was still blowing, and patted the seat next to her.

"Mum, this is bonkers! You'll get the sack! Why don't you just talk to me at home like normal people?"

"Guess I'm not normal then," she said.

"No," I said. "No." I was still trying to whisper. Mrs Gold was pretending not to listen but I bet that woman could read lips ten miles away, old-lady glasses or not. "You're not normal! Our family's not normal, our family's rubbish!" I was so angry I wouldn't have been surprised if steam was coming out of my ears.

Mum reached for me and I pulled away.

"You think you're going to make it better like this?" I said. "Well, it's already ruined, everything is ruined."

"It's all right, love...."

"No, it's not!" I wasn't going to cry. "It's not!"

"I'm sorry, love," Mum said. "I've been on a bit of

157

another planet. But we're not rubbish... I'm so proud of you."

"She is, you know," Mrs Gold said. "I've seen you with the boys... you're a diamond."

"Yes, Seren," Mum said. "You are."

"They hate me, they all hate me. Sasha hates me and now Keith hates me... and Christina's hated me for months...." I was breathing fast and shallow and for some reason I couldn't quite work out, my vision was a bit blurry.

"I'm sure they don't, love." She patted the seat next to her again and I sort of fell into it.

Mum took a deep breath and held my hand. This time I let her. "Last week I saw Christina's mum in the market. I felt such an idiot! I didn't know... I didn't know about you two falling out," she said. "And so long ago! Oh, Seren, why didn't you say anything? You know you can talk to me...."

"When? When can I talk to you? There was always stuff. Stuff going on." I shrugged. "And that's been ages. Old news. I am totally over it." I sniffed.

"I felt so bad... hearing it from her," Mum said. "And so sad for you, you two were so close. Sisters, I always said, you and Christina, Sash and Fay. Like an extra family. Oh, love, I'm so sorry. People change, friendships change." She was quiet for a bit.

"I know that! I know all that about growing up and moving on. I do read magazines, you know."

"I'm sorry I wasn't there for you, Seren."

"Well, you never are, you're always off in some dream world. You never notice anything real, not with me or even when it happens to Sasha!"

She held my shoulders and looked at me, suddenly scared. "What's happened to Sasha? Oh my God, what is it?"

"She's not pregnant, Mum. This isn't one of your books, this is real life. Haven't you noticed she's not been around? I mean, she's supposed to be doing her GCSEs but you don't seem to care at all!"

Mum hugged me close, but I pushed her away.

"'Course I care!" Mum said indignantly. "I just thought... you know, she needed some space. I mean, our house, it's like a bloody tornado goes through every five minutes. I thought she needed some quiet. Everyone needs quiet sometimes."

"I don't. I want our house full again. I want Sasha talking to me. I want Sasha telling Denny to shut up...."

"Sasha's not talking to you?" There were tears in her eyes and she sniffed.

"You never knew! That's what I've been saying, you don't know anything!" I said, and the tears started. I let Mum hold me close. "You never listen when it's just me. Never. You're always tired, and it's always me sorting the boys. I'm not a childminder, I'm thirteen! It's always me making things nice and smooth, and no trouble, and it's not fair!"

"I'm listening now, love, honest." She stroked my hair. "I'm here now."

I put my head against her even though I was as tall as she was, and I breathed in the smell of warm bus, of crisp packets and people and a little bit of petrol and my mum, then I cried some more.

When the tears had stopped a bit I told her all about everything. About Christina who wasn't my friend any more, and Sasha who wasn't my sister, about Denny being too big for his boots and calling me his half-sister, and Arthur playing up because he never got enough attention. About how I had been really worried Dad would go to Cyprus and I'd never see him again, but then I was wrong, about how Nene hated me, about how I wanted to do Drama and Gamze and Ayshe did it but didn't care, and it was not fair. About falling over in front of the whole school and feeling clumsy and useless. And then I told her about how, just when I thought I was doing something right, I ruined Keith's film and now I had no friends at all.

Mum held me tight and rubbed my back.

When I did open my eyes, Mrs Gold was looking at me from the priority seats. "Oh, you'll be fine, Seren," she said. "We all mess up, don't we, Linda?"

Mum smiled. I could tell from her eyes that she had been crying too. "I'm sorry, love. Really I am," she said. "I'll cancel my library ticket. I'll do less hours."

"No!" I said. "Don't cancel your library ticket. Just put the book down. Sometimes. OK?"

"OK," Mum said.

It was a long time before we got home, past eleven o'clock. Mum drove Mrs Gold right home to her front door. Mrs Gold promised she'd do anything it took to get my mum out of trouble, even writing a letter saying that it was her fault Mum had stopped the bus because she'd had some sort of funny turn. Mum said thanks and they hugged, and Mrs Gold told me to be good. Then Mum drove us back to the garage.

"Does this count as stealing a bus?" I said. "Do you think you'll really get the sack?"

"I hope not," Mum said, as she went in to talk to her manager. "Keep your fingers crossed for me. Maybe you should lend me your lucky eye."

I said I didn't think it would help, so I just gave her a hug and waited. I couldn't hear what they said in the office, but Mum was in there ages, and once or twice there were raised voices. I sat on the plastic seat and thought that nothing much changes really, that even though Mum wasn't at school she still had loads of people telling her this and that, and you just have to take it.

Keith was right, the only thing you can do is be cool.

Keith. I shivered. He hated me. I shut my eyes and turned the lucky eye over and over.

Mum had called Sasha to come home and sit with the boys, and I suppose she thought she was cleverly fixing things so we'd have to talk to each other. Mum didn't say that as we walked home, but I guessed it was what she was thinking. It was good walking with her in the dark, and I couldn't remember when we'd last even been out together, except to see *Spongebob Squarepants* last summer holidays with the boys.

"I know I've been working loads," Mum said as we turned into our estate. "I thought, no, I *know* it's the right thing. We need the cash." She took my hand. "People like us, Seren, don't have a lot of choices. Four kids!" She looked at me. "It's not just hard, it's expensive."

"I know that!" And I was proud of her. "I know you work hard, Mum. We all do."

"I couldn't manage without you, you know that." Her eyes were shiny.

"Stop the love fest now!" I said. "Before one of us starts blubbing all over again!"

★★★

The house was dark, but Sasha's shoes were in the hall. I saw my reflection in the hall mirror and I looked exhausted from all that crying and talking.

"Do you want to see if Sasha's still up?" Mum said. "I could make some hot chocolate and we could sit on the sofa with the duvets?"

We hadn't done that for years, all of us, even the boys, on the sofa or lying on the rug with the duvets. It made me smile for a second. But I thought of Keith and tomorrow, and even though I knew I'd be lying in bed thinking of any kind of way I could make things up with Keith, I wanted to be in my room, in my bed. I rubbed my eyes. "I got to text Keith," I said.

"If there's anything I can do, you know, I could always talk to Wendy?"

Wendy was Keith's mum. Keith's mum probably didn't know anything about the film and would be pretty happy to learn that the whole project had gone so wrong. After all, as far as Keith's mum was concerned, Keith was still on the fast track to accountancy.

"S'all right," I said. And I kissed her good night.

Upstairs, Sasha was reading a text book in bed with headphones on. I hadn't seen her, not properly, since the day in the costume cupboard. I turned away.

No, I thought. I saw her with Jamie Kendrick and then I made Keith run and then I lost his film and then.... I sat down on the bed, facing away from Sasha, and took off my lucky eye. I checked my phone for messages. Nothing. I texted him again. SRY SX.

I heard Sasha take her headphones off, and the buzz and squeak of R'n'B coming out of the tiny speakers for a few seconds before she turned her music off. Her bedside light clicked off, and the room was lit orange from the street-light outside.

I changed and slid into bed. It was quiet. Outside somewhere, a helicopter chopped through the sky, and a police siren whizzed along the main road.

"Seren?" Sasha was saying my name.

I thought I'd imagined it for a minute. Then she said it again and I turned over.

"Seren, I'm really sorry."

I put my hand out of the bed and she caught it in hers and squeezed. I felt her fingers, her funny double-jointed thumb, the ring she'd got from her nan. There was a lovely warm feeling bubbling up inside me.

"Is this... did Mum put you up to this?" I said. Although, I thought, I wouldn't have cared if she had.

"No!" she said, and I could tell from her voice that it was true. "Look, this isn't about Mum." Sasha paused. "Seren, I'm sorry. I can see it now, all that stuff in the supermarket, I know it was daft. But I know you were trying to help. I mean, Jamie talked to me, Jamie Kendrick. You've got him to thank, really."

"I have?"

"Yeah, Jamie." I looked across at her, and even though it was dark I could see her face so happy when she said his name. "He made me see you were sticking up for me. He said he'd have done the same thing if I was his sister."

"He did?" I said and squeezed her hand back.

"Well, maybe not tried to set her up with Luke Beckford," she said.

"No." I said in a quiet voice. "But I was only trying to help...."

"I know," she said. "I shouldn't have listened to Fay. Christina's not a big fan of yours. I'm sorry. It was when I put that picture up on the net and I read those things they said. I knew it had all gone too far. I mean, it's one thing me slagging you off, but seeing all those other people going at you... urgh... you didn't deserve that."

"You did it?" I said.

"Sorry. Jamie said I should apologise. He said I was lucky to have a sister who'd fight for me. I'm sorry I was mad about the job too. Your dad called, he explained it." Another pause. "I'm sorry. I am the biggest idiot."

"Second biggest," I said. I smiled. We were still holding hands. It felt so good.

"So," I said. "You and Jamie then? Not Luke?"

"Luke! He thinks he's so it! I am definitely over him. Totally. He's only started going with Keisha Coates again. And Jamie is way cuter than Luke, believe! And about a million times sweeter...."

I wondered whether I should tell her I saw them

that afternoon… it seemed like weeks, or even months ago.

"So, you do forgive me, Seren, don't you?"

I tried to stay cool. "Only if you pick the boys up from school sometimes. Oh, and do the teas and help more with the shopping."

"I've got exams!"

"You'll manage!" I said. "I had a talk with Mum. Some of us need to help out a bit more."

"Is that what happened on the bus tonight?"

"How do you know?"

"Carol from the buses called and was asking about it. She said Mum was for it…. She hasn't got the sack, has she?"

I told her the whole story. I told her about the film too.

"Yeah, Fay was telling me her sister should have been in it."

"Yeah, well if Keith had any sense he should have stayed well away from me."

"No!" Sasha said, "You're a million times better at acting than Christina. She looks like one of those dummies in a shop window. I mean have you seen what she does with her hands?"

"You noticed too?"

"Can't help it," Sasha said. "Anyway, of course Keith would want you in it, even without the acting, I mean, Keith's practically family."

"Not any more. I ruined it. Not ruined it, lost it. All his work down the drain."

"What did you do?"

It came out then that I'd seen her and Jamie, and that I'd been so scared of Sasha seeing me that I'd run.

"So it was my fault, sort of," Sasha said. "Can't he do it again?"

"He wanted to get it into this competition. I don't know if there's time... Sasha, it was my fault, and he hates me."

"I hated you!" Sasha said. "And I don't now."

"That's different," I said.

It was quiet. The alrm clock ticked. We lay there in the dark holding hands across the gap in the beds.

"I need to make it up to him," I said.

"So why don't you film the stuff you lost?"

"You don't understand, Sasha. Keith's got the school camera, and he's got the 'eye'. That's what Miss Tunks said."

"OK," said Sasha. "I've got a camera on my phone... and between us we've got plenty of eyes! We should

168

do it, Seren. This weekend. Tomorrow! Jamie can help, he did a video for media studies."

"I don't know..." I said. "A phone? The quality would be rubbish, wouldn't it? Keith would laugh at us."

"Not if we did a really brilliant job," Sasha said. "I'll text Jamie now." She pulled her phone from under her pillow. "We'll have it sorted by Saturday afternoon."

12

ARTHUR'S WINGS

On Saturday morning the sun was out and everything was looking up. Sasha was speaking to me and the boys were almost behaving. I was still trying to forget that Keith hadn't returned my calls or texts. But apart from that, it was as perfect as it gets, which is always a sign that it won't last long.

It didn't.

The phone went and I pounced on it, hoping for Keith, but getting instead Straggly-beard Man, who leads Denny's choir, calling to remind him about a big all-day rehearsal in the Olympic stadium itself. Denny pointed out it was on the calendar, and Arthur started up saying he wanted to go to the Olympic stadium over and over again.

"You'll have to take me, Seren," Denny said.

"Why me? I can't, Sasha and me, we've got stuff to do."

"I want to go to the st-a-d-i-um," sang Arthur.

Mum came downstairs in her dressing-gown and, amazingly, took control. I thought I must have woken up in a parallel universe. She told Denny she'd already done a packed lunch and that they'd be leaving in an hour.

"And me, and me!" Arthur was jumping up and down. I knew it wouldn't work. I imagined Arthur running wild around the Olympic site, causing Gold Medal chaos. I could see Mum was thinking this too.

"You girls can look after Arthur," Mum said.

"But we're filming!" I said.

"I don't wanna go with girls!" Arthur said.

Mum made a 'please' look at me and Sasha. "We'll do a proper old-fashioned Sunday dinner tomorrow, all of us."

I gave Mum a look that said Yorkshire pudding hadn't done it for me since I was seven.

Arthur was jumping up and down, singing, "Gravy! Gravy!"

"But you have to go with the girls, love, just for today." Mum knelt down and held Arthur by the shoulders and looked into his eyes. "Art," she said. "I'm sorry, you can't come with me and Den. There's only a pass for one to go in with Den, that's it. Arthur, you have to be really good and really grown-up for me." She looked across at me and Sasha. "You too."

I knew she was right. But I knew it was going to make things a lot harder.

★★★

We swung by Jamie's and picked him up, and me and Arthur walked behind Sasha and Jamie.

Arthur said, "Is it allowed for someone that tall to go out with Sasha?"

"Yes," I said.

"Then it's OK for Keith to go out with you even though he's smaller than you?"

"Arthur, you know Keith's like my extra brother," I said.

"He is fun though, more fun than Denny."

I had tried to call Keith loads, but it was ten now and I knew he'd be off at Chinese Saturday School, and then Youth Orchestra. Keith would be cool, wouldn't he? I took a deep breath, I really wasn't sure.

We got to the café, and compared to the weekday it was crowded. It still wasn't full, but half the tables had people having their morning coffee. Worst of all, Nene was hovering by the entrance to the kitchen.

I swear her face sort of curled up when she saw us.

"Hello, Nene," I said, nice and polite, remembering that very soon, in a month or two, I would never have to see the woman again in my whole entire life. "Is Dad around?"

Nene shouted in Turkish into the kitchen and Dad appeared, flustered but less worried.

"Seren, Babes! Sash and... Denny?"

"No! I'm Arthur!"

"But you've grown so big," Dad said with a smile. "I thought you must be Denny!"

Arthur glowed with joy.

"Sasha! I'm sorry. You see how we suffer without you? If I could afford it I'd have you back like that." He snapped his fingers.

Nene rolled her eyes and crossed her arms more firmly. She muttered in Turkish and although I had no idea what she was saying I could tell she wasn't dishing out the compliments.

"And who is this young man?" Dad said.

Jamie Kendrick put his hand out to shake Dad's.

"Jamie Kendrick, Mr Ali."

"Sasha's friend," I said.

"Sasha's boyfriend!" Arthur said.

We explained about the filming, and Dad was cool,

but there was no way we'd get the same effect with the low light and the camera on the phone which, however much Sasha and Jamie tried to big it up, was not a patch on the school one.

Arthur didn't help. "I'm bored," he said. "I'm going outside with Mehmet."

Jamie and Sasha filmed me in tight close-up so we didn't get any of Nene moaning on in the background, or the other diners. I tried to look lost and, what was the other word? Disorientated. But then Arthur was leaning against the plate-glass window making faces and squashing his nose flat, and it was so disgusting I just burst out laughing.

Then Nene started getting really angry, yelling at Arthur through the glass and then at me, looking me up and down as though I was skankier than dog poo.

"S'all right," I said to her coolly, "I'll have a word."

Nene had a look on her face like she'd swallowed something gross, but I ignored her and went outside and talked to Arthur. I looked back into the café. Jamie was filming us. I waved and Arthur waved too.

"Look, just be good," I said to him. "Be good for five minutes, then I'll get my dad to bring you an ice cream, OK?"

"OK." Arthur nodded. "But she scares me." He pointed inside to Nene.

"Yeah," I said, "you and me both."

Jamie showed me the film of Arthur, and somehow, through the plate-glass with the light behind him, Arthur looked completely angelic, like a curly-haired spirit, or a sprite.

"Oh My God!" I said. "Ariel!"

"What?" Jamie and Sasha said together.

"Wait here. Dad, can you get these two a coffee, and an ice cream for Art? I just got to do something."

I ran down the street to the party shop on the corner of Dalston Lane and bought the boysiest pair of fairy wings they had. They were white and silver, and I wondered how I was going to make Arthur wear them, given that he would have finished the ice cream by the time I got back to the café.

"Arthur," I said, out of breath. "Put these on."

He gave me a look.

"Wear these, and I'll make Keith put you in the film," I said. I had my fingers crossed behind my back. Keith might not even talk to me again.

Arthur put his head on one side. "Will it be like Kutest Kiddie?"

"No, nothing like that," I said. "A million times

better than that. And if Keith wins you might get to be on the big screen at the Rio. Ten foot tall!"

This was true. But it did rather depend on Keith talking to me again, and then liking what we were doing, and finally, winning.

"Like Godzilla!" Arthur said and put on the wings there and then.

I made him stand outside and put his hands flat on the glass and look in. He looked like a child ghost, fuzzy and unreal.

Keith would love it.

Jamie let me film it while he and Sasha had another coffee, and gazed into each other's eyes. I wished Keith was here to see this. I would have phoned him if he hadn't been sitting in a hall in Soho talking Chinese.

Nene was humphing at me all the time, and I was glad we were nearly done.

"Thanks, Dad." I hugged him just before we left.

"No problem, Babes." He ruffled my hair. "Come back soon. You too, Sasha."

"Goodbye, Mo," Sasha said to my dad. Then she turned to Nene, hands on hips. "You know, you think we don't get what you're saying all the time? Well, we may not get the words, Mrs Ali, but your tone is crystal clear. And you know what? Now I'm not working here, I can safely say you are the rudest old lady I have ever met! You don't deserve a granddaughter like my sister, Mrs Ali." Sasha took Jamie's arm and walked out.

My mouth must have been flapping open, I was so stunned. I'd so always wanted to say that.

Nene erupted in a volcano of what I bet was classic Turkish swearing.

"Ohmigod! Sasha!" I put my hand over my mouth to hide my smile, and ran out after them. "She always thought we were the family from hell. Now I bet she's sure of it."

"That woman!" Sasha said. "She slags you off something rotten when you're not around, and I bet she was doing it just now, in Turkish. All those sly little looks. You deserve better. I'm not having someone bad-mouth my sister, even if I can't understand what she's saying."

I hugged Sasha hard. It felt so good to have a sister again.

★★★

We got to the estate and filmed a bit more, with me and with Arthur as Ariel, leading me through the concrete and out to the canal. As we walked along the towpath, we could see the stadium, and Jamie said how he and his football team were doing a display in there, and how much he was looking forward to it.

"Have you been inside yet?" I said.

"Nah... it's not been open to the public," he said.

"Denny's in there today," Arthur said. "He's in there with Mum."

"Do you think we could get in?" I said. "If we could film me in the dress, and Arthur in his wings inside the site, Keith would be so impressed...."

"Would he like that?" Arthur said.

"Yeah, I think he would."

"Well, come on." Arthur pulled on my arm. "Let's have a look then."

The main entrance was so wide you could have driven two lorries through it sideways. The 'Avenue of Champions', Jamie said the school coach had called it, planted with spindly, brand-new trees. But there was a gate, or not so much a gate but one of those poles that comes down, and a guard in a box.

It was obvious he wasn't going to let anyone through.

Sasha did her best. "It's my brother, he's singing in the rehearsal." She looked at her watch. "We were supposed to meet him inside." She had her worried face on.

The guard wasn't having it. "Sorry, love. Passes only."

Sasha stuck her bottom lip out so far you could have used it as a bookshelf for really heavy books. "Please?"

The guard turned away and went back inside his box. Sasha shrugged.

Arthur was hanging on the pole, still wearing his wings.

"Film that, Jamie," I said.

The guard noticed his pole wobbling, and then noticed Jamie filming, and was suddenly out again. "No filming on site."

"It's only a phone."

"And you!" He was shouting at Arthur. "Stop that, now!"

The guard started walking towards Arthur, and Arthur jumped down off the pole and ran. Straight down the Avenue of Champions towards the stadium.

"Arthur!" I said.

"Go after him!" Jamie whispered. "Go on!"

The guard was talking into his radio and Arthur was disappearing away down the main road. I ducked under the pole and legged it after him, and caught hold of him just in time.

"Arthur! What are you doing? They could have tazers or anything!"

I could see a sort of golf buggy thing with guards heading towards us so I pulled Arthur along and ran back towards the entrance and under the pole. Then Jamie scooped Arthur up and we didn't stop running until we'd made it over the little bridge across the canal and back into the estate.

Mum and Denny were already back, sitting in the front room eating pizza in front of the telly.

"There's some for you in the oven," Mum said. "Denny was fab, weren't you, love? And the stadium! You should've been there! Anyway," she went on, wiping her fingers on a bit of kitchen roll. "What have you lot been up to? You look like you've escaped from the circus!"

All four of us were red in the face from running and laughing, I was wearing the grey spangly dress over my school trousers, and Arthur had on a pair of white and silver wings.

I turned my phone back on after we'd eaten the pizza. I'd had it turned off most of the day because of the filming. There were about a million messages and texts, all from Keith. I read the first one. SRY, it said. The second one said, REALLY SRY.

The third one, FOUND MMRY STK SRY AGN.

The tenth one said, TALK TO ME PLS!!!!!

I was so happy I almost pressed redial right away. But then I had a much better idea.

I downloaded what we'd filmed on Jamie's phone, and sent it to Keith on the computer, and then went straight round.

He was sitting on the wall outside his shop, waiting.

"Did you see it?" I said. "Have you seen it?"

"The memory stick? I'm really sorry. It was in the bag all the time. I am an idiot."

"Yes," I said. "So is the film all there? Everything, the stuff in the Cave?"

Keith nodded. He put out his hand for me to shake, but I bent down and hugged him until he almost choked.

"You're OK? You're not mad with me?" Keith said. "Only I felt so down last night, and then this morning when I emptied my bag... I should never have blamed you."

"No," I said. "But it's OK now. We're OK."

"Yeah," Keith said. "We are." He smiled and pushed his glasses up his nose and I hugged him again.

I was fizzing with excitement. "But have you seen what we did today? I sent it to you. I think you'll like it.

We shot it on Jamie Kendrick's phone and Arthur's Ariel and everything!"

He was smiling as much as me.

The day flashed by inside my head. Sasha, Arthur, Keith. I felt so lucky.

13

SUMMER TERM

It was only the second week of the summer term, but the Year Elevens had had their Leavers' Prom and left school for study leave before their exams. It seemed like such a long time had passed, although I still shuddered if I thought about me in the *Paradise Supermarket* yelling 'slug-brain' at Luke Beckford.

Sasha was still going out with Jamie, and happier than ever. She'd even got a new job in the cinema tearing the tickets. Denny's head wasn't getting any bigger, because now the opening ceremony was coming closer he was getting seriously jittery. Mum had sorted her shifts so she did more 'earlies' and we'd already had two brilliant picnics, one in Greenwich Park with Jamie and Keith along too.

Me and Keith were cool. I was so relieved I hadn't lost the oldest mate I had. And even though he found the memory stick, he still used some of the phone-filmed stuff because it looked so good. He loved Arthur as Ariel too, said it was a brilliant idea. Said he told me I always had good ideas.

Keith had done all the editing and sent it off, and a letter had just come saying he was on the shortlist. Our film was on the shortlist!

Everyone who saw it liked it, Miss Tunks included. She said Keith was fantastic and I was 'very convincing'. I heard her talking in the corridor to the head of English – Mr Josephs – and she said she thought Keith could win! I hadn't told him that yet, though, in case his head swelled up so big he wouldn't be able to walk through any doors.

Just for the record, I was one hundred per cent sure he would win, and so was Sasha.

Arthur had decided he was a star and persuaded Mum to let him go to Drama class at the Arcola. He went to the tiny class. I got into the senior class. I was babysitting for Sherifa once a week and paying for me and Arthur together (there was a reduction for more than one family member). Drama class was one of the best decisions I ever made. It was really good fun. I loved it.

Me and Keith had started another film, this time

with talking. There were two of my mates from Drama class in it with me, Jade and Becky, and I was trying not to get too excited about it.

So, me and Keith were sitting in the dinner hall and he was talking about how he needed to get the school camera over the weekend. We were just about to go when Miss Tunks came past. I almost got up too quickly and missed her tray by millimetres.

"Seren Campbell Ali!"

"Sorry, Miss Tunks," I said, going pink.

"Miss Tunks," Keith said. "About the camera...."

"Fine, fine." She waved a hand. "I'll be in the Drama office just before lessons start this afternoon. Oh, and Seren," she said, looking at me. "I've got something you might be interested in."

"Me?" I said. I couldn't think that I'd done anything wrong.

Miss Tunks rolled her eyes. "Yes, you! Honestly, Keith, sometimes I think your friend is scared of me or something."

Me and Keith looked at each other.

"It's about the National Youth Theatre," Miss Tunks said. "It would be a very good thing for you. Who knows where it could take you?"

"Me? I thought you thought I was rubbish!" I said.

I wasn't sure if I had just thought the words, but then I realised I must have said them out loud, from the way Miss Tunks sighed and looked at me.

"No, Seren, you are very talented. Really. I think you should audition."

"Yes, Miss Tunks," Keith said, nodding and smiling at the same time. "I think she should too."

CATHERINE JOHNSON

is an award-winning writer
of Welsh/African-Caribbean descent,
living in the East End of London. Her novels for
children include *Stella, Landlocked, The Dying Game,
Arctic Hero*, selected for Booked Up 2009,
and *A Nest of Vipers*, short-listed for the UKLA
Award 2009. She also wrote the screenplay for
Bullet Boy, the 2005 film about British gun crime,
starring Ashley Walters. She lectures in Creative
Writing at London Metropolitan University,
and is a member of the 2012 Olympics Committee
responsible for choosing medals. Catherine works
regularly with children and teachers in schools
and libraries across the UK. *Brave New Girl*
is her first book for Frances Lincoln.